THE FAIRY SWARM

THE IMAGINARY VETERINARY: BOOK 6

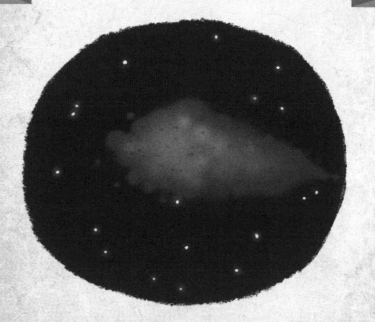

BY SUZANNE SELFORS
ILLUSTRATIONS BY DAN SANTAT

Little, Brown and Company
New York Boston

For fairies everywhere

Text copyright © 2015 by Suzanne Selfors
Illustrations copyright © 2015 by Dan Santat

Little, Brown and Company

Hachette Book Group
1290 Avenue of the Americas, New York, NY 10104
Visit us at lb-kids.com

Little, Brown and Company is a division of Hachette Book Group, Inc.
The Little, Brown name and logo are trademarks of Hachette Book Group, Inc.

The publisher is not responsible for websites (or their content) that are not owned by the publisher.

First Paperback Edition: May 2016
First published in hardcover in October 2015 by Little, Brown and Company

The Library of Congress has cataloged the hardcover edition as follows:

Selfors, Suzanne.
The fairy swarm / by Suzanne Selfors ; illustrations by Dan Santat. — First edition.
pages cm. — (The imaginary veterinary ; book 6)
Summary: "Ten-year-olds Ben Silverstein and Pearl Petal have had quite a busy summer as apprentices of Dr. Woo, veterinarian for imaginary creatures. When a swarm of sugar fairies escapes into Buttonville, Ben and Pearl must protect the townspeople, keep the fairies safe, and outsmart the dangerous poacher, Maximus Steele"—Provided by publisher.
ISBN 978-0-316-28693-0 (hardcover) — ISBN 978-0-316-28695-4 (ebook) —
ISBN 978-0-316-28694-7 (library edition ebook)
[1. Fairies—Fiction. 2. Imaginary creatures—Fiction. 3. Veterinarians—Fiction.
4. Apprentices—Fiction.] I. Title.
PZ7.S456922Fai 2015
[Fic]—dc23

2015005806

Paperback ISBN 978-0-316-28692-3

10 9 8 7 6 5 4 3 2 1

RRD-C

Printed in the United States of America

CONTENTS

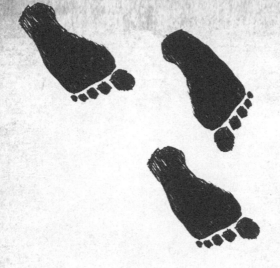

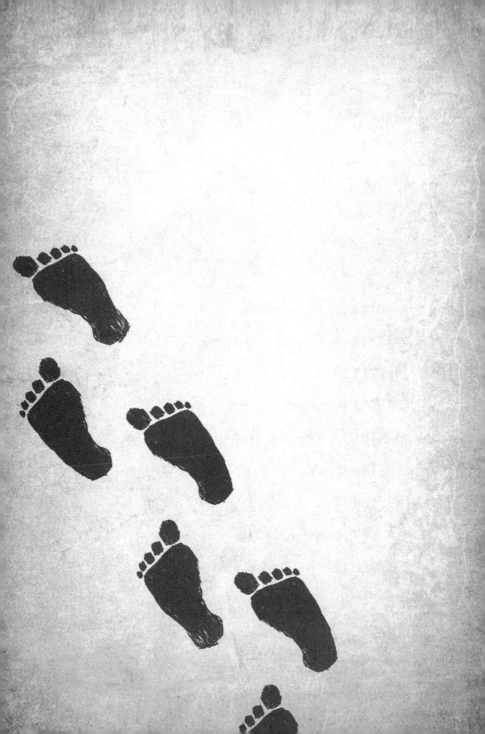

1

SWEETNESS AND LIGHT

On the first Saturday of every month, Pearl Petal and her great-aunt Gladys ate breakfast together at the Buttonville Diner. It was a tradition of sorts. "A couple of nice gals out on the town," Gladys always said, though sometimes she couldn't remember Pearl's name. Because the elderly woman insisted on bringing her two wiener dogs, it took an extra-long time to walk the half block from their building to the diner, which annoyed Pearl, who liked to walk as fast as possible. But the wieners stopped to piddle on *everything*, and to smell *everything*, and to bark at EVERYTHING. Pearl vowed to never, ever own wiener dogs.

When they finally reached the diner and stepped through the front door, Pearl's impatience melted away. Her nostrils inhaled the scents of cinnamon rolls warming under the heating lamp and bacon sizzling on the grill. "Yum. Let's eat!"

"Come along, Sweetness and Light," Gladys said as she pulled her dogs inside. The wiener dogs waddled across the checkered linoleum and barked at the waitress. Then they barked at Mr. Bumfrickle, who was sitting at a table by himself, eating a bowl of oatmeal and reading the newspaper with a magnifying glass. They also barked at Ms. Bee, Pearl's teacher from last year, who sat at the counter, eating a waffle.

No one told Gladys that her dogs weren't allowed inside. Buttonville was one of those small towns where everyone knew everyone else. Thus it was well known that wherever Gladys went, so, too, went her annoying little yappers. The waitress, whose name was Lucy, pulled a pair of high chairs over to Gladys's favorite booth. Pearl strapped each dog into a chair, securing the trays so the dogs could rest their little front paws. The dogs stared at the door and growled softly as if they were expecting an invasion.

"Will you be having the usual?" Lucy asked as she filled Gladys's mug with coffee.

"Usual for me," Gladys replied.

"Me too," Pearl said.

"Hey, Lionel!" Lucy yelled. "They're having the usual!"

"You got it!" Lionel yelled back. He was the fry cook, and his apron was covered in greasy stains.

As Lucy began clearing another table, Gladys opened her purse and took out her knitting needles. Even though her fingers were knotted with arthritis, she was always working on a project. Almost everything she wore that morning had been knitted by her own two hands—her pink vest, her green skirt, her orange hair bow. She even made stuff for her dogs. "Don't you love their breakfast hats?" she asked Pearl.

"Super cute," Pearl said with a forced smile. The hats were white with yellow blobs on top, just like fried eggs. Because Sweetness and Light were shaped like sausages, the theme kind of made sense.

Gladys sipped her coffee, then her needles began

to click and clack. "How is everything with you, dear?"

This was a big question because things with Pearl were, well, *extraordinary*. All summer long, she'd been working as an apprentice to Dr. Emerald Woo, veterinarian for Imaginary creatures. Thus far, she'd met a dragon hatchling, a sasquatch, a lake monster, a leprechaun, a black dragon, a rain dragon, a unicorn king, a unicorn foal, a kelpie, some satyrs, a royal griffin, and a man who was actually a shape-shifting cat.

But weeks had passed and Pearl hadn't met any new creatures, nor had her fellow apprentice, Ben Silverstein. And though she hated to admit it, she'd grown a bit bored with scrubbing scales off the floors, dusting fur from the walls, and changing various litter boxes. There'd also been lots of sasquatch grooming. Because the sasquatch's fur was prone to tangles and mats, it needed brushing almost every day. And it had recently become a fan of yoga, which meant that Pearl had to learn poses such as downward-facing dog and warrior two. But

while she and Ben had gone about these mundane tasks, they'd wondered about things. How come no calls had come in from the Imaginary World? Why had no trips been taken? And when would they meet another creature?

"Everything with me is fine," Pearl told her great-aunt. "I really like working at Dr. Woo's Worm Hospital."

"Worm hospital," Mr. Bumfrickle mumbled. "Who ever heard of a worm hospital?" He turned the page of his newspaper. At that sound, the wiener dogs perked up their ears and barked. Mr. Bumfrickle scowled at them. "Can't a man eat in peace?"

Gladys soothed her dogs, then took another sip of coffee. "How is that nice friend of yours? Oh dear, I can't remember his name."

"You mean Ben Silverstein? He's fine." Pearl tapped her fingers on the table. Where was Ben this morning? She looked out the window. Nothing much was happening on Main Street. Across the way, Mr. Wanamaker, the barber, was sitting outside

his shop, waiting for customers. Up the street, her parents were inside the Dollar Store, also hoping for customers. Ever since the old button factory closed, it had been tough to make a living in Buttonville. Even the cinema had trouble staying open and showed movies only on Friday nights and the occasional matinee. The current movie was an old-timey black-and-white thing.

INVASION OF THE KILLER BEES

SPECIAL SHOWING 4 PM THIS SUNDAY

Pearl wondered if she and Ben should go see the movie. Killer bees could be interesting. And the popcorn was pretty good, even though the cinema used butter flavoring instead of real butter.

Zzzzzt.

A bug flew around the wiener dogs. They started barking like crazy. Then it flew straight at Pearl. "Go away," she said, swatting at it with her hand.

"I hope you're not talking to me," Lucy said with a smile as she set two plates on the table. "The usual."

"Thanks." Pearl swatted at the bug one more time before it flew away.

Pearl's stomach grumbled with anticipation as she grabbed her fork. She'd ordered the number six on the menu, which was two buttermilk pancakes, two strips of bacon, and two scrambled eggs *well done*, because runny eggs were disgusting. Her great-aunt Gladys had ordered the number eight, a mound of mushy corned beef hash, from the senior menu, which meant it cost less. Gladys set her knitting needles aside and spooned some hash onto the wiener dogs' high chair trays. While Sweetness and Light snorted and snuffled the food, Pearl made a sandwich with her pancakes.

Zzzzzt.

★8★

The bug was back. It zipped around the waitress's head. "Oh, that looks like a nasty hornet," Lucy said. "I hate those things."

It whipped around Ms. Bee's head. "I don't think that's a hornet," she said as she ducked. "It's too big."

It swooped past Mr. Bumfrickle. "You got bugs in this restaurant," he complained. "I'm gonna call the health department."

"Now, now, don't be getting upset over one little bug," Lucy said. "It'll go away."

But the bug didn't go away. It flew around Pearl's head, then hovered over the syrup bottle. The dogs kept on barking. Aunt Gladys leaned over and snatched the newspaper from Mr. Bumfrickle, rolled it up, aimed, and—*whap!*—corned beef hash scattered across the table.

"You missed," Pearl reported. "Here, let me try." She grabbed the newspaper. All it would take was a quick whack and she'd be able to enjoy her breakfast. That pancake sandwich was going to be delicious. The bug flew around Aunt Gladys, then

dive-bombed Pearl's plate, grabbing a little piece of syrup-covered pancake. With its treat in hand, the bug landed on the windowsill. Pearl raised her arm, aimed, and...

The little creature turned its face and looked up at her.

Pearl gasped and dropped the newspaper. Ms. Bee was right. That thing was *not* a hornet.

2

QUEEN BEE

Pearl scooted out of the corner booth and yanked the magnifying glass from Mr. Bumfrickle's hand. "I need to borrow this," she said. There was no time to be polite. This matter had to be dealt with *immediately*.

"What's going on?" Mr. Bumfrickle complained. "Can't a man enjoy his breakfast in peace?"

While the dogs barked and Mr. Bumfrickle muttered to himself, Pearl scrambled back into the booth. The creature was still standing on the windowsill, eating its prize. Carefully, so as not to startle it, Pearl lowered the magnifying glass. Then she peered through the lens. "Holy guacamole," she whispered.

It was definitely not a hornet. Nor a bee of any kind. Pearl knew this because she'd studied them in biology class last year. Ms. Bee had a special fondness for bees, on account of her name, and she kept a tray of specimens in her desk drawer. Whether a wasp or a nasty hornet, all bees possessed the following things: segmented bodies, little fuzzy insect legs, and furry insect faces. This creature had a tiny human body, two human legs, and a smooth human face. The only things it had in common with a bee were wings and antennae.

"It's a fairy," Pearl said with a delighted squeal. Then she cringed. She shouldn't have said that out loud. But fortunately the wiener dogs were barking so obnoxiously that no one in the diner had heard Pearl's declaration.

"Now, now, Sweetness and Light. Momma won't let the bad bumblebee hurt you." Gladys spooned more hash onto their trays. With tails wagging, the dogs slurped up their food.

Pearl scooted closer to the windowsill, holding the magnifying glass as steady as possible, despite her trembling hand. The fairy looked like a girl, with tangled hair as green as spring leaves and skin as brown as tree bark. Perched upon her head was a little silver crown. A rush of excitement filled Pearl's entire body. She felt as if she might faint. "It must be a princess. Or a queen," she said, once again much louder than she'd intended.

Ms. Bee, who was seated at the counter, pivoted on her stool. "Did you say a *queen?*" She pointed her fork at Pearl. "Better be careful. If the queen is here, that means she's looking for a new place to nest. The rest of the hive will follow."

"We can't have a hornet nest in the diner," Lucy said as she filled a ketchup container. "Hurry up and squish that thing!"

Kill it? No way! "Don't worry," Pearl said. "I'll take care of it." She needed a container. After setting the magnifying glass aside, she grabbed a saltshaker, unscrewed its little lid, and emptied the contents into an empty coffee mug. The fairy was busily munching on some pancake, so she didn't seem to notice the glass container hovering above her head. "Easy," Pearl whispered. "Easy." Then, quick as a wink, she set the saltshaker over the fairy.

"What's going on?" Mr. Bumfrickle hollered, smacking his hand on the table. "Where's my newspaper? And my reading glass? Dadburnit."

The fairy dropped her piece of pancake and began pounding on the wall of the shaker. It looked as if she was yelling, but the glass muffled the sound. As the fairy flew around the inside, still pounding her fists, Pearl raised the shaker ever so slightly and slid a napkin underneath. Then, with her hand cupped over the napkin, she tipped the saltshaker so it was right side up. As the fairy tumbled to the bottom, Pearl removed the napkin and quickly screwed the top back into place. It was a perfect fairy container because it already had little holes in it for air. "Gotcha," Pearl said proudly.

Ms. Bee had been watching with interest. "Let me take a look," she told Pearl. "If it's the queen, then I'd love to keep it as a specimen for my class."

Pearl pictured the fairy skewered onto Ms. Bee's velvet display board between a black beetle and a monarch butterfly. "Uh, I was wrong. It's not a queen." Holding the shaker in both hands, Pearl slid out of the booth. "Gotta go," she said as she hurried toward the diner's door, her blond ponytail swishing. "Thanks for breakfast!" Before her great-aunt could ask any questions, and before Lucy, Ms. Bee, or Mr. Bumfrickle could get a better look at the amazing creature she'd caught, Pearl made her escape.

"Best get rid of it!" Ms. Bee called. "Or the swarm will follow!"

Pearl hadn't taken a single bite of her number six, but she didn't care. *I found a fairy*, she sang to herself. *A fairy, a fairy, a FAIRY!*

She needed to tell Ben. He'd be so amazed. He might be at his grandfather's house, or at the

★15★

Buttonville Senior Center, where he sometimes volunteered. She'd check those places first. She was about to run up Main Street when a flash of red caught her eye. "Drat," Pearl grumbled. *Archenemy alert!* Victoria Mulberry, dressed in her usual overalls, was walking straight toward her.

It was tough being a kid in Buttonville, mostly because there were very few choices for friends. Victoria Mulberry was the only other girl who was Pearl's age. It would have been nice for both girls if they'd become best friends. They could have worked on school projects together. Spent birthdays together. Gone to the Milkydale County Fair together. Unfortunately, Victoria was not a free-spirited, fun-loving, adventure-seeking sort of girl. Victoria was a persnickety, tattle-telling, whiny, spoiled, mean, unpleasant sort of girl. And while some say that opposites attract, that was far from the truth with Victoria and Pearl.

The saltshaker vibrated in Pearl's hands as the fairy flew around. There were no pockets in Pearl's

shiny blue basketball shorts, so she clasped her hands behind her back. "Hey, Victoria," she said, trying to sound as bored as a brain cell in Victoria's brain.

"I'm not talking to you," Victoria announced as she stopped right in front of Pearl.

"Fine by me," Pearl said, which was the truth, because any day spent not talking to Victoria was a good day in her book.

Victoria's red hair was so frizzy it looked as if she'd stuck her finger into a light socket. "Don't you want to know why I'm not talking to you?" She glared through her thick glasses.

"No, I don't." Pearl shuffled in place. The salt-shaker tickled her palms. "And by the way, you *are* talking to me. Just thought I'd point that out."

"I'm too busy to talk to you because I've got some important reading to do." Victoria held up a rather thick book. This was not unusual. She almost always carried a book. What *was* unusual was that she was walking alone, without her mother, and without her red wagon.

Pearl glanced at the book's title. *History of Dragons* by Dr. Emerald Woo. "Where'd you get that?" Pearl asked with a gasp. She'd seen a copy of the book before, but it was owned by Metalmouth, the dragon who lived on the hospital's roof. How had Victoria found it?

"Ever since I saw that dragon, I've wanted to learn more about them," Victoria explained. "So I went to the bookstore, and Ms. Nod special-ordered this for me. I didn't know Dr. Woo was a writer."

It was true that Victoria had seen Metalmouth. But Pearl and Ben would never admit to knowing a dragon. Or a sasquatch. Or any of the other creatures they'd met over the summer. They'd each signed a contract of secrecy for Dr. Woo, and they would never break it. "You're still talking to me," Pearl said snidely.

"I saw it," Victoria said, spit flying off her blue braces. "I'm going to learn all about dragons, and then I'll know exactly how to find it. And when I do, I'm going to take a picture and send it to the *Buttonville Gazette*." She tucked the book under her arm. "What's that sound?"

High-pitched buzzing began to stream from Pearl's clutched hands. It was as if a tiny storm had been unleashed inside the saltshaker, as the fairy continued to fly round and round. Pearl shrugged.

"Whatcha got behind your back?" Victoria tried to dart around Pearl, but Pearl was quicker on her toes. "What's in that saltshaker?"

"I caught a..." Pearl glanced across the street, at the cinema's marquee. "A *killer* bee."

Victoria recoiled. "Oooh! I'm allergic to bees."

That was the best news Pearl had heard all day. "It's a big queen killer bee," she announced. "I'm thinking of setting it free." With a squeal, Victoria hurried away. "Nice talking to ya," Pearl called.

Pearl checked the status of her captive. The fairy had stopped flying. She stood on the floor of the saltshaker, folded her arms, and glared at Pearl. "Sorry," Pearl said, "but I can't let you go. Not yet."

Then she remembered her mission—to find Ben and share her amazing discovery. She turned up Olive Street, then took a left on Cedar, and spotted him right away.

"Ben!"

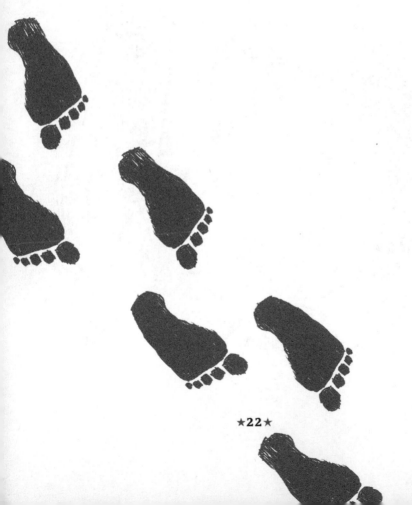

3

ANOTHER SECRET

Ben and his grandfather Abe Silverstein were walking down the front steps of the Buttonville Synagogue. "Hi, Pearl," Ben called with a wave. Both he and his grandfather were each wearing a blue yarmulke—a small, flat hat—on the crown of their heads.

"Hello, Pearl," Grandpa Abe said. His eyes twinkled beneath his bushy gray eyebrows. Despite the warm summer weather, he'd buttoned his wool cardigan all the way up to his chin. "What a nice Shabbat service. Why don't you join us next week for kiddush?"

"For what?" Pearl asked.

"It's like snack time, after services, when we say the blessings over the bread and the grape juice," Ben explained.

"Sure. That sounds nice." Pearl held the saltshaker behind her back. "Uh, can I borrow Ben, please?"

"Off for another adventure?" Grandpa Abe asked. Pearl nodded. "All right, already. You kids go have fun." Ben took off his yarmulke and handed it to his grandfather. "But remember, boychik, I need your help later at the senior center. We've got to set up for pudding day." He ruffled Ben's hair. Then, with his cane tapping the sidewalk, Grandpa Abe ambled toward his old Cadillac.

Pearl grabbed Ben's arm and hurriedly led him around back, where an alley ran between the synagogue and the Buttonville Bakery. The scent of cinnamon wafted from the bakery's open window. "Look!" She shoved the saltshaker in his face. "I caught her at the diner!"

"Her?" Ben scratched his head.

"Yes. I think it's a *her*. She's wearing a little dress."

"A dress?" Ben pressed his nose against the glass, going cross-eyed as he stared at the tiny creature. The fairy folded her arms and stuck her tongue out

at him. He gasped. "Whoa! Is that a...?"

"Yep." Pearl smiled so big the gap between her teeth showed.

They'd shared this sort of moment before—discovering the dragon hatchling, finding the sasquatch, and encountering Metalmouth. But no matter how many creatures she met, the thrill, excitement, and awe had never gone away. And no matter how many secrets she and Ben shared, they'd never broken the contract of secrecy.

"Where'd you find her?" Ben asked.

"She was flying around the diner. She ate part of my pancake." The fairy shook her fist at them. "We can't let you out," Pearl told her. "It's against the rules for Imaginary creatures to leave Dr. Woo's hospital." Pearl and Ben had learned this rule back when the sasquatch escaped. The fairy stomped her foot and started yelling again. She seemed super angry.

"If she came to Buttonville to see Dr. Woo, that might mean she's sick," Ben said. "We'd better take her to the hospital."

"Now?" Pearl asked sadly.

"Yes, now. What else would we do?"

"Well, I was kinda hoping I could keep her for a little while." Pearl hugged the saltshaker to her chest.

Ben frowned. "You can't be serious."

But Pearl was serious. She loved fairies. Ever since her very first day as Dr. Woo's apprentice, she'd been hoping to meet a fairy, and now she had one in her hands. The fairy didn't seem happy about being trapped, but Pearl was confident that once they got to know each other, they would become best friends. And besides, she'd done a real good job taking care of Lemon Face, her pet parakeet. Surely she could take care of a fairy.

Always the voice of reason, Ben put a hand on Pearl's shoulder. "What if she needs medicine? What if Dr. Woo's worried and looking for her?"

"But—" Pearl sighed. As much as she wanted to keep the creature, she didn't want to be responsible for a fairy not getting her medicine. "Drat," she said softly. "I hate it when you're right."

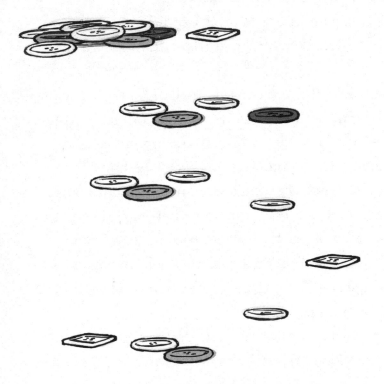

4

A wrought-iron fence and padlocked gate enclosed the hospital's property, but Pearl and Ben knew a secret place where they could climb over. As soon as their feet hit the ground, they hurried across the overgrown lawn and up the hospital's front steps. As usual, the note taped to the door read:

THE WORM HOSPITAL IS **CLOSED** UNTIL IT IS **OPEN.**

Pearl had done her best not to jostle the fairy. She'd walked with extra-long strides, trying to keep her footsteps from bouncing. And before climbing the fence, she'd reached through the bars and had carefully set the shaker on the ground so it would be safely waiting for her on the other side. But despite Pearl's attempts to make the fairy comfortable, the little creature was still throwing a tantrum— pounding on the glass and shrieking like a rabid mosquito. "I'm sorry," Pearl told her. "We're almost there."

While Pearl held the shaker, Ben knocked. And knocked and knocked. There was no sound of approaching footsteps. No dead bolts sliding open. He pressed his ear to the door. "It's quiet in there."

"Knock again," Pearl said. Ben did, and when nothing happened, Pearl hollered, "Mr. Tabby! Mr. Tabby!" But still no one answered.

Perhaps Metalmouth was home. During the day, the dragon was often asleep in his nest on the roof. Pearl hurried down the front steps and stood in the middle of the yard. She cupped her hands around her mouth and called, "Metalmouth! You awake? Hey, Metalmouth!" But no reptilian face appeared at the roof's ledge. Her arms dropped to her sides. "Where is everyone?" she asked Ben.

"Maybe they're out back," Ben suggested.

"Oh, good idea."

As they walked around the building, Button Lake came into view, glistening in the morning sun. The dock was empty, as was the yard. The lake monster had returned home a few weeks ago, so there were no ripples on the water. Pearl turned around and looked at the hospital's back windows. Dr. Woo's office, on the second floor, was dark. Her gaze traveled to the third floor's Forest Suite.

"Hey, sasquatch!" she yelled. "We need to get in!" But no furry face appeared. She craned her neck, looking all the way up to the tenth floor, where Violet and Vinny worked the switchboard. That floor was also dark.

"We could crawl in through one of the broken windows," Pearl suggested.

Ben shook his head. "I don't think we should do that. That's called breaking and entering, and it's against the law."

"But the window's *already* broken," Pearl pointed out. "We'd just be entering." Then she sighed. For the zillionth time, Ben was right. The apprentices were only supposed to be at the hospital on Mondays, Wednesdays, and Fridays. Entering without an appointment or invitation was definitely against the rules. And Mr. Tabby took rule-breaking very seriously.

"This seems weird," Ben said worriedly. "Do you think something's wrong? Where did everyone go?"

Pearl had no idea. "I'm guessing that's why the fairy was flying around Buttonville. She couldn't find anyone inside the hospital."

The fairy pressed her nose against the salt-shaker's glass and stared up at the building. "We could let her out. Then she could fly through the window and wait for Dr. Woo," Ben suggested.

"Maybe, but what if she doesn't? What if she

flies back to Buttonville and gets lost? Or goes back to the diner and gets squashed by a rolled-up newspaper?"

Ben cringed. "Gross." He stuck his hands in his pockets. "I guess you'll have to take care of her until Dr. Woo or Mr. Tabby comes back."

Pearl was happy she got to keep the fairy a bit longer, but a nagging thought kept her from smiling. What if something was wrong and the creature needed medical attention? "We'd better leave a note for Dr. Woo."

It took a bit of time to figure out how to leave a note, since neither Pearl nor Ben was in the habit of carrying paper or a pen. But the old button factory still had a mailbox outside the front gate, and it was overflowing with junk mail, much

of which had fallen onto the sidewalk. Ben reached
his arm through the bars and grabbed a flyer.

The back of the flyer was blank, perfect for writing a note. Ben rummaged around the junk mail until he found an envelope from a bank advertising its lending rates. There was a free pen inside. "What should I write?" he asked.

Pearl dictated.

Dear Dr. Woo and Mr. Tabby,

I found a fairy. I think she's a girl, and I think she might be important because she's wearing a crown. I'll take her home and hide her in my bedroom. When you get back, please come and get her. I live above the Dollar Store on Main Street.

Your loyal apprentice,
Pearl Petal

P.S. Don't be afraid if you hear barking dogs. They make a lot of noise, but they won't attack you.

Ben slid the note under the front door. Then he gave Pearl a serious look. "You sure you can take care of her?"

Pearl hugged the saltshaker again. "I've waited my whole life to meet a fairy," she said. "I'm sure I can do this. Dr. Woo will be very proud."

5

FAIRY-SITTING

Pearl Petal had a fairy in her room.

Her dream had come true. "Woo-hoo!" Pearl was so excited she jumped on her bed for ten whole minutes. "This…is…so…amazing!" The fairy sat at the bottom of the saltshaker, on the dresser, watching Pearl go up and down. After a few more jumps, Pearl sprang off the end of the mattress and landed on the carpet. Then she grabbed a magnifying glass.

Luckily, the Dollar Store carried the plastic lenses. After saying good-bye to Ben, who was off to help his grandfather at the senior center, Pearl had snatched one from aisle three. And she'd managed to hide the saltshaker from her parents, sneaking it upstairs into her bedroom. "I'll be down soon to do my chores," she'd called to her mom and dad.

"Okay," Mr. Petal had called from the front picture window, where he and Mrs. Petal were creating a new window display of plastic picnic supplies.

Because she didn't have to worry about being interrupted, Pearl could finally take a longer look at the little creature. Holding the magnifying glass next to the shaker, she examined her catch. The fairy sat cross-legged with her wings folded and a big frown on her face. "Can you understand me?" Pearl asked. The fairy nodded. "Please don't be mad," Pearl said. "I need to keep you safe until Dr. Woo gets back. Everyone at the diner wanted to squish you. And Ms. Bee wanted to pin you to a board in her classroom." The fairy stuck out her tongue. *Yeesh.* There was just no pleasing some people.

The fairy was almost exactly like the drawings

Pearl had seen in storybooks. Her dress was made of tiny yellow flowers. Her shoes had been cut from shiny green leaves, and her crown had been woven from silver sticks and red berries.

"I like your green hair," Pearl told her. "Mine turned green last summer 'cause there was a lot of chlorine in the public pool. It's closed now. If you want to go swimming around here, you have to use the plastic pool at the senior center." The fairy strummed her fingers, as if bored. Pearl decided to change the subject. "Why were you flying around the diner?"

The fairy opened her mouth, and a stream of squeaks rose from the saltshaker's holes. "I'm sorry," Pearl told her. "I can't understand you. Maybe I should just ask you yes-or-no questions. Did you come to Buttonville to see Dr. Woo?" The fairy nodded. "Are you sick?" The fairy shook her head. Pearl let out a big sigh of relief. That was excellent news. "But why would you come to see the doctor if you aren't sick? Oops, that's not a yes-or-no question." Pearl fidgeted. "Are you hungry?"

The fairy jumped to her tiny feet.

Pearl knew that the fairy liked pancakes with syrup. So, saltshaker in hand, she opened her bedroom door and crept to the kitchen. The coast was clear. Her parents were still working downstairs. Pearl grabbed a frozen waffle and popped it into the toaster. The fairy watched. When the waffle was golden brown, Pearl poured syrup on it and cut off a tiny piece. Carefully, she began to unscrew the saltshaker's lid, intending to quickly slip the morsel inside. But as soon as the lid was loose, the fairy's wings unfurled. She zipped to the top of the shaker and began pushing. "Hey!" Pearl said. "Stop that!" Pearl quickly screwed the lid back into place. *Phew!* Close call.

The fairy hovered inside the shaker, pointing at the syrup bottle. "You want syrup?" The fairy nodded. Pearl tipped the bottle over the saltshaker. A droplet oozed through a hole and landed on the saltshaker's floor. The fairy knelt and lapped it up like a cat. When she was finished, Pearl squeezed another droplet, which was also quickly eaten.

Wow, she sure likes sugar, Pearl realized.

"You thirsty?" The fairy nodded again. In went a couple drops of orange soda, followed by a drop of honey. Pearl wondered if the glass bottom would get sticky, but the fairy ate every last bit. The glass

was so clean it sparkled. Then the fairy curled into a ball and closed her eyes.

Pearl put her ear to the saltshaker's holes. She could barely hear the soft snoring sounds. *Perfect timing*, she thought. *I've got chores to do.* Even though the fairy was deep asleep, maybe in a sugar-induced stupor, Pearl wondered if she was comfortable. Cold glass was not the best material for a bed. So Pearl got two squares of double-ply toilet paper, carefully opened the lid, and dropped them in. *Those should make nice blankets.* After replacing the lid, she hid the shaker in her bedroom closet, then hurried downstairs to help her parents with the window display.

Before, during, and after dinner, Pearl made sure to check on the fairy, who had rolled herself up in the toilet paper like a caterpillar in a cocoon. "As soon as Mom and Dad go to sleep, I'll feed you again," Pearl whispered. Pearl's bedtime was 9:00 PM. She took her shower, brushed her teeth, and put on her blue pajamas. Then she slipped under her quilt. "I'm ready!" she hollered.

"But it's only eight thirty," Mrs. Petal said. "Are you sick?"

"No. I'm just tired." In an attempt to be convincing, Pearl forced a yawn. "Maybe we should all go to bed early. What do you think?" The sooner her parents went to bed, the sooner she could talk to the fairy. While Pearl couldn't understand the fairy's squeaks, she could at least ask questions that required a nod or a shake of the fairy's head. And Pearl, being a girl who loved to ask questions, had a lot of them stacking up. She yawned again. "Good night."

"Come to think of it, you did work hard on our window display," Mr. Petal said. "It makes sense that you'd be extra tired."

Mr. and Mrs. Petal tucked Pearl in and kissed her good night. But they didn't go to bed. Instead, they cleaned the kitchen, watched TV, and sat at the table, paying bills. Pearl stared at the closet door. She didn't dare bring out the fairy. Her mom often checked throughout the night to make sure

Pearl wasn't reading by flashlight or leaning out the window, counting stars. It wasn't until ten thirty that she heard their bedroom door shut and their light click off. *Finally!*

Pearl threw the quilt aside. To avoid squeaky floorboards, she reached under her bed and grabbed her special pink slippers. A gift from Cobblestone, a leprechaun she'd met at Dr. Woo's, they gave her the ability to walk in silence. She put them on, then made her way across her bedroom as quiet as a ghost.

Tap. Tap. Tap.

Pearl stopped dead in her tracks. A huge face was peering through her bedroom window. Red eyes glowed like fire pits. Steamy breath fogged up the glass pane. Pearl slid the window open. "Metalmouth?" she whispered. "What are you doing here?"

"Hiya, Pearl," Metalmouth said in his rumbly dragon voice. He was standing on the roof of her building, but he'd stretched his long neck to reach her window.

"Shhhh," she scolded. "Mom and Dad are asleep."

His ears flattened. "Sorry." He wasn't very good at being quiet. Dragon voices weren't designed for libraries or midnight clandestine activities.

"You shouldn't be here. Someone might see you."

"Nobody's gonna see me. I'm the same color as night." He stuck his head into the bedroom. So much steam wafted from his nostrils that Pearl's room started to feel like a sauna. "Do you wanna play fetch?" He spat a yellow tennis ball onto the carpet. The ball glistened with spit.

Playing fetch was one of Metalmouth's favorite activities, along with welding metal into pieces of art, but there was no time to do either of those things. Pearl glanced nervously at her door. If her parents saw the fairy, she could easily pretend it was some sort of bug. But there'd be no way to pretend that a dragon was anything but a dragon! "Metalmouth, did Dr. Woo read my note? Does she know I found a fairy?"

"Yup, she knows. That's why I'm here." Metalmouth scratched his chin on one of Pearl's bedposts. "Dr.

Woo wants to see you right now. And the fairy, too."
His ears flattened again. "I don't like fairies. They
bite." It was funny to think that a creature as big as
a dragon could be afraid of an itty-bitty fairy. But
Metalmouth wasn't your usual storybook dragon.

"Did you say *right now*?"

"Uh-huh. I already got Ben."

"You got Ben?"

"He's on the roof."

"How'd he—?" Pearl narrowed her eyes. The
Dollar Store building was two stories high, plus a
basement, but there was no fire escape ladder. If
Ben hadn't climbed to the roof, then that meant...
"You flew him up there?"

"Sure I did. And I'll fly you to the hospital if you
want. Or you can walk. But Dr. Woo said you gotta
come now." His tongue darted out and grabbed the
tennis ball.

Fly or walk? Why had he even bothered to ask
such a ridiculous question? Pearl walked every single day of her life. *Forget that!*

She could sneak out. But if she did, and her parents woke up and looked for her, they'd panic. And she'd get into the biggest trouble ever. "I can't leave without telling my mom and dad. Give me a few minutes. Then I'll meet you on the roof."

As she hurried down the hall, she had no idea what she'd say. Too bad she didn't have time to talk to Ben. He was way better at making up stories. She knocked on the door, then opened it. "Hey, Mom, Dad, you still awake?"

Mrs. Petal bolted upright and flicked on the bedside lamp. "What's going on? Are we having an earthquake?" Mr. Petal, who wore earplugs to bed, kept snoring.

Pearl fidgeted in the doorway. "Uh, Dr. Woo just called. She needs my help."

Mrs. Petal glanced at the clock. "At this hour? But it's the middle of the night."

"It's an emergency. A bunch of worms are sick. They have...uh..." She'd watched Ben tell some weird stories. But no matter how crazy the story

sounded, Ben always acted as if it made total sense. "It's a worm disease...and it's called...ringworm. Yep, they've got ringworm."

"That's odd," Mrs. Petal said, rubbing her eyes. "I thought ringworm was something that people got."

"Well, worms get it, too. And if it's not treated, it could spread to all the worms in Buttonville. And that would be a disaster of epic proportions," Pearl said with a dramatic sweep of her arms. "So I'm going to help, okay? Because I'm her apprentice and she needs me."

"I don't want you walking in the dark alone," Mrs. Petal said.

"I won't be alone. Ben and Dr. Woo's assistant are waiting for me." Metalmouth was kind of like an assistant, she figured.

"All right. I guess it's okay, as long as you go with them. I'm very proud of you for being so dedicated to your job." She blew Pearl a kiss, yawned, then turned out the light.

Back in her room, Pearl opened the closet and grabbed the saltshaker. The fairy popped her head

out of the toilet paper cocoon and started yelling again. Even after a nice sleep, she was still cranky.

"Calm down," Pearl told her. "I'm taking you to Dr. Woo. And guess what?"

The fairy fell silent. Pearl smiled.

"We get to go by dragon!"

6

THE RED-EYE FLIGHT

Pearl was in such a hurry to fly on a dragon that she forgot all about changing her clothes. Luckily, it was a balmy summer night, so her pajamas and leprechaun slippers were plenty warm. Saltshaker in hand, she opened the hatch that led to the roof.

It was nearly impossible to see up there. The streetlamps weren't working. And the moon was currently on the other side of the earth.

"Hello?" Pearl whispered. "Where are you?"

"Over here." A streak of orange light suddenly appeared, guiding the way. While dragon flame can burn a village and melt a bridge, it can also serve as a convenient torch. Pearl crossed the roof and joined Ben, who was also in a pair of pajamas and sneakers. His pajamas were yellow, and his sneakers hadn't been made by a leprechaun.

Metalmouth closed his mouth, extinguishing the flame, and Pearl's vision began to adjust. That was when she noticed the red saddle strapped to the dragon's back.

"Did you really ride here on Metalmouth?" Pearl asked.

"It was amazing," Ben said in a hushed voice. "He tapped on my bedroom window. The cat went nuts."

"Did you tell your grandpa you were leaving?"

"No. Luckily he didn't wake up. But I left a note for him next to the box of doughnuts. He has one every morning, so he'll find the note for sure." Ben pointed to the saltshaker. "How's the fairy?" The

creature was flying around, screaming again. It sounded as if Pearl had trapped a miniature storm.

"She's not very happy," Pearl said with a frown. "I don't think she likes me."

"Well, you did trap her."

"Hey, you guys, we'd better go," Metalmouth said. "Dr. Woo's waiting."

"I can't believe this is happening," Pearl said with an excited giggle.

Metalmouth lay on his stomach and stretched out a wing so Pearl and Ben could climb easily onto his back. Pearl settled in the front of the saddle. The seat was padded and quite comfortable. Ben sat behind her.

"Just in case you're wondering, there aren't any helmets," Ben informed her. "Or seat belts. I already asked."

"You don't need that stuff," Metalmouth said as he rose onto his paws. "No one's ever fallen off, except for that one time when Mr. Tabby fell into the lake. Gee whiz, he was mad. Cats sure hate water." As he spread his wings, a piece of roof tile tumbled to the sidewalk. Way down in the basement apartment, wiener dog barks arose.

"Uh-oh. Sweetness and Light will wake up the whole neighborhood," Pearl said. "We'd better get outta here."

Metalmouth perched on the edge of the roof and began flapping his wings. "Hold on super tight," Ben warned, his arms wrapped around Pearl's waist. "He flies really...*fast!*" With a sudden lurch, they rose into the sky. For a moment, Pearl forgot to breathe. She couldn't speak. She squeezed the saltshaker so tightly her hand began to ache.

Metalmouth flew up Main Street, then dipped his wing and banked to the right, carrying them over the company houses, where Grandpa Abe lived. Barnaby, Abe's black cat, stood on the front porch. His back arched when he spotted the huge scaled beast. A pair of raccoons darted behind a garbage can as the dragon's shadow swept across driveways and lawns. Cold night air stung Pearl's eyes, but she didn't care. A fairy in one hand, a dragon saddle in the other—what could be better? (Perhaps

a not-so-cranky fairy would make things a tad bit better, but Pearl wasn't going to fuss over details.) She squealed with joy as Metalmouth finished the 180-degree turn.

"Hey, isn't that Victoria?" Ben said.

While other Buttonville residents were snug in their beds, Victoria Mulberry stood in her backyard, gazing through a telescope, watching the night sky. *She's looking for dragons*, Pearl realized. But before she could warn Metalmouth, he flew straight over Victoria. The telescope toppled as Victoria screamed. Then she ran into her house, most likely to get a camera, or worse—her mother. Luckily, Metalmouth headed toward the forest, dipping behind the tree-tops, out of view.

"We're gonna need a real good cover story," Ben said.

"Don't bother," Pearl hollered over her shoulder. With the wind in her ears, Pearl found it was difficult to hear. "Victoria already knows Metalmouth is real. There's nothing we can say to change her mind."

The dragon's red eyes glowed like headlights, illuminating a path through the darkness. Soon, the towering, old button factory came into view.

The building looked eerie at night. All the windows were dark except for Dr. Woo's office on the second floor. With a thud, they landed on the roof. Metalmouth galloped past a few chimneys, then skidded to a stop.

"Wow, that was fun!" Pearl exclaimed as she climbed off. "Can we do that every night? Can you take us up through the clouds, like an airplane?"

"Sure," Metalmouth said. "But clouds make me sneeze."

"If we go again, I think we should get helmets, and maybe parachutes, just in case." Ben swung his leg around and slid off the saddle. "Goggles would be nice, too." Pearl didn't think any of that safety stuff was necessary, but if she ever took a longer trip on Metalmouth's back, she'd recommend a saddle that reclined and a cup holder.

"Eh-hem." The sound of throat-clearing drew their attention to the rooftop door, where Mr. Tabby, dressed in his usual perfectly ironed trousers, crisp dress shirt, and vest, was waiting. "Do not dawdle. We have important matters to discuss," he said, his voice as serious as ever.

Metalmouth plucked his tennis ball from behind one of his scales. "Wanna play a game of fetch when ya get done?"

"Sure," Ben said. "See you later."

"Yeah, see ya," Pearl said.

"Okeydokey." The dragon sat on his haunches and began to untie the saddle.

Mr. Tabby's mustache twitched, and he sniffed the air as the apprentices approached. "Do I detect the sugary odor of fairy?"

"Yes," Pearl said, holding up the saltshaker. The fairy started pounding on the glass again. "Should I let her out?"

"Under no circumstances are you to release her," Mr. Tabby said. "Not until Dr. Woo deems it safe. There is no knowing what mischief she might get into. Fairies are notorious troublemakers."

Troublemakers? Pearl smiled. For a moment,

she cherished the discovery that she and the fairy
had something in common. Almost everyone in
Buttonville thought of Pearl as a *troublemaker*. But
the fairy didn't have the same reaction. She stomped

her foot, then began tearing up the toilet paper in a fit of rage.

"She's mad at me because I've kept her in this shaker all night," Pearl explained. "I didn't know what else to do. We came to the hospital, but no one answered the door. Where were you? Did you go to the Imaginary World? Did something happen? How come the fairy's in Buttonville? Did you know that she likes pancakes with syrup? Do—" Mr. Tabby raised a hand to shield himself from the questions, as if they were little spit wads shooting from a straw.

"Enough," he said with a low growl. Now that Pearl knew he was a bakeneko, a shape-shifting cat, she'd begun to notice more of his feline tendencies. "Dr. Woo, Metalmouth, and I were not at the hospital because we were on a quest. That is all you need to know." His half-moon irises flashed. Then he held the rooftop door open and ushered the kids through. "Let us not keep the doctor waiting."

7

Pearl and Ben had been to Dr. Woo's office a number of times, so they were not surprised to find it cluttered as usual. Crates and boxes were stacked randomly. Weird things floated in jars. There were skeletons and fossils, feathers and shells, and books. Lots and lots of books.

Dr. Woo sat behind her massive, carved desk. Her long black hair cascaded over the shoulders of her white lab coat. Despite the late hour, she was wearing her work clothes, just like Mr. Tabby was. Pearl no longer stared at the scars on the doctor's face and neck. They now seemed as normal as freckles.

"Sorry to get you both out of bed," she said as she took a sip from her coffee mug. "Did you enjoy your ride?"

"Oh yes!" Pearl said. "It was the best ever."

Ben nodded enthusiastically. Then he added, "But a seat belt would have been nice. There were a couple of times when I thought I might slip off."

"Good to know." Dr. Woo took another sip, then set her mug aside. "So, where is she?" Pearl placed the saltshaker on Dr. Woo's desk. "I assume you'd like to be released," Dr. Woo said to the fairy. The fairy jumped up and down. "Do you promise to be good?" The fairy nodded. "Mr. Tabby, will you please secure the door?" He closed the office door but remained there, as if guarding it.

Pearl and Ben watched eagerly as Dr. Woo slowly unscrewed the saltshaker's lid. As soon as it was removed, the fairy unfurled her wings and popped out the top as if jumping off a trampoline. Then she zipped around the room so fast she was nothing

more than a blur. Even though it was difficult to see her, there was no avoiding her piercing, high-pitched whine. She whipped around Dr. Woo, Mr. Tabby, and Ben. Then she came straight at Pearl.

"Ouch!" Pearl cried, grabbing her earlobe. "She bit me!"

"You are lucky she only bit you once," Mr. Tabby said. "She appears to be enraged."

"But I was just keeping her safe," Pearl explained. The fairy hovered in front of Pearl's face, motioning wildly with her arms and hands. "Now what's she doing?" Pearl asked.

"Most likely she is trying to turn you into something unpleasant," Mr. Tabby said. "A toad, a bat, or a flea, perhaps."

"A flea?"

"Don't worry," Dr. Woo said with a dismissive wave. "Fairy magic will not work in the Known World."

"That's good news," Pearl grumbled as she rubbed her throbbing earlobe. But it didn't seem fair that the creature was mad at her when she'd simply been trying to help.

The fairy landed on the desk and kept squealing. Dr. Woo sighed. "Mr. Tabby, would you please turn on the translator?"

Mr. Tabby pulled out his creature calculator, a

device he used when identifying, treating, and locating various creatures. He set it next to the fairy, then pushed a button. Immediately, the squealing was absorbed into the device, then shot back out in words they could understand.

"Mean girl, mean girl, put me in a bottle! Mean girl, mean girl, her throat I want to throttle!"

Pearl gasped. "Is she talking about me? I'm not mean. I gave her a waffle and syrup."

"She's the worst. I'll make her cursed!" The fairy waved her arms again, but nothing happened. "Oh, hummingbird poop!" she said with another foot stomp. "Magic be gone." She rose into the air and flew at Pearl again. But before she could bite Pearl's other ear, Dr. Woo grabbed a little net and caught the fairy in midair. Then she dumped the fairy back into the saltshaker and tightened the lid.

"We do not bite the apprentices," Dr. Woo said, shaking a finger at the glass. "You will stay in there until you settle down." Dr. Woo walked around the desk and examined Pearl's ear. "It's just a surface wound. You'll be fine. But I am sorry she bit you. Sugar fairies are known to have quick tempers, and they express themselves with a great deal of emotion."

"Sugar fairies?" Ben asked.

"Yes, but don't let the name fool you. They may eat sweet things, but they lack a sweet nature." Dr. Woo raised an eyebrow. "And this sugar fairy, in particular, has an *extra*-bad temper."

"You know her?" Pearl asked.

"Certainly." Dr. Woo picked up the shaker. "Pearl, Ben, I'd like you to meet Twanabeth Twilight, my missing apprentice."

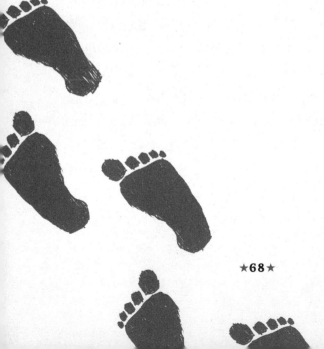

8

THE FOUND APPRENTICE

Pearl and Ben had heard a little about the missing apprentice. She'd held the job before they did, but she had apparently forgotten to punch her time card one day, and no one knew where she'd gone, or whether she was in the Known World or the Imaginary one. Both Ben and Pearl had thought this odd. A missing kid was a very big deal. But Mr. Tabby and Dr. Woo hadn't seemed worried.

Now it made sense. The apprentice wasn't a missing *human*.

"The missing apprentice is a fairy," Pearl said with awe.

"That's right." Dr. Woo grabbed a pair of reading glasses from her desk, slid them onto her face, then peered through the saltshaker at Twanabeth. "And from the looks of that crown on her head, I'd guess she's recently become the queen. Is that true?" The fairy nodded. "Did the old queen die?" The fairy hung her head. "I'm sorry to hear of your loss."

"How come you didn't know the queen had died?" Ben asked the doctor. "Don't you talk to the fairies?"

"Rarely," Dr. Woo said. "We're not allowed into their realm in the Tangled Forest. They don't like tres-passers, and they use magic to protect themselves. If they need care, they come here. We've created a spe-cial room for them on the fifth floor." Neither Pearl nor Ben had been to the fifth floor. Pearl instantly wanted to run up there and check it out.

"Set me free! Set me free! Out of this bottle, I want to be!" Twanabeth pounded on the glass.

Dr. Woo set the shaker on her desk. Then she folded her arms and spoke sternly. "I will let you out, but you must promise to stop biting." The fairy nodded.

"This should help." Mr. Tabby pulled a packet from his pocket. It was labeled: KIWI-FLAVORED JELLY BEANS. He set one of the little green beans on the desk.

"Excellent idea," Dr. Woo said. She opened the shaker. Pearl grimaced and covered both earlobes, expecting to be attacked at any moment. But when Twanabeth flew out, she ignored Pearl and landed next to the bean. As she bit into the sugary green candy shell, her wings folded and a happy humming noise filled the room.

"Sugar fairies love sugar," Dr. Woo explained. "Best we let her finish. It might help her mood."

While the fairy munched, Ben settled onto a crate, then rested his elbows on the desk. Pearl sat next to him. Twanabeth ate quickly, consuming the entire bean, which was as big as her torso, in a matter of seconds.

Mr. Tabby set a second bean on the desk, and she ate that one, too.

"Whoa," Ben said. "She should enter one of those eating contests. Does she like pies? Or hot dogs?"

The fairy burped. Having finished her snack, she looked around, then pointed at Pearl. "It is very mean to capture the fairy queen," she said.

"I'm sorry," Pearl told her. "I was just trying to help."

Mr. Tabby glanced at his pocket watch. "The hour is late. Perhaps our guest could tell us *why* she is here."

Twanabeth began jumping up and down. "He's bad. He's bad. He makes me mad!" Her little crown toppled off her head.

"Who's bad?" Ben asked. "She's not talking about me, is she? I didn't do anything to her."

Dr. Woo removed her reading glasses and sighed. "I'm afraid she's speaking of Maximus Steele."

At the mention of that horrid man, Pearl's entire body stiffened. Oh, how she hated him! Maximus

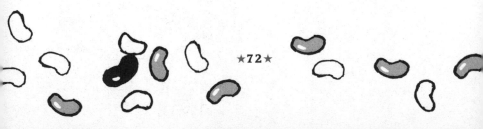

★72★

Steele was a poacher who had sneaked into the Imaginary World. He'd taken one of the rain dragon's horns, he'd tried to trap a unicorn foal, and he'd fooled the griffin king into believing he was trustworthy. Unfortunately, he was still there, and no one knew which creature he'd target next.

Dr. Woo and Mr. Tabby shared a long, concerned look. "Twanabeth, has Maximus invaded your realm?" the doctor asked.

Twanabeth grabbed her crown and plunked it back on her green hair. "Maximus is bad for us. He wants our dust! He wants our dust!"

Dr. Woo sank into her chair. "I thought there'd be more time to prepare. If he's entered their realm, then that means he needs fairy dust."

Pearl frowned. Fairy dust, a substance that looked like yellow glitter, was used for travel between the Known World and the Imaginary World. Dr. Woo needed a constant supply so she could help the creatures. But if Maximus Steele got a supply, he could bring Imaginary creatures, or their horns and

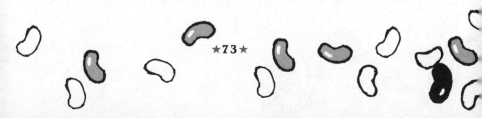

tusks, into the Known World and sell them. Then he'd surely reach his goal of becoming the richest man ever.

As Dr. Woo slumped in her chair, she suddenly looked very tired. Her shoulders deflated, and the scars on her face and neck seemed darker. Pearl had never seen her look so worried.

Mr. Tabby strode to the window. With his hands clasped behind his back, he gazed at the night sky. "This is very bad news," he said. "If Maximus has invaded the fairy realm, he will do whatever it takes to force the fairies to surrender their dust."

Twanabeth flew across the desk, the tips of her feet skimming the wood, and stopped in front of the doctor. "I am the queen, this be true, and I no longer work for you. But your help I need! Your help I need! To hide my people until our world is freed."

"You want the fairies to come here and hide?" Ben asked.

"Oh, that's a great idea," Pearl said excitedly. Even though her earlobe still ached, she was pretty sure not all the fairies would dislike her. She'd make

certain not to put any of them into saltshakers. "How many are there?"

"Of the sugar variety, there are hundreds," Mr. Tabby said.

"There are other kinds of fairies?" Ben asked.

"Certainly. Burrowing fairies, they live underground. Bat fairies, they hang upside down when they sleep. And worker fairies, the Portal captain is one of those. And there are wingless fairies, too, such as the leprechauns."

Pearl looked at her slippers, remembering Cobblestone. "Do they all make dust?" she asked.

"We are dust! Dust is us!" Twanabeth chanted.

"Only sugar fairies make the yellow dust that powers the Portal," Mr. Tabby explained. "They shed it, the way we shed skin cells."

Ben tapped his fingers on the desk. "So if Maximus got hold of a sugar fairy, he could collect the dust and ride the Portal whenever he wanted."

"Correction, he could *summon* the Portal whenever he wanted," Mr. Tabby said. "He would still require a pilot. Or he would have to fly it himself."

"I saw him flying a giant moth," Pearl said. "Is that anything like flying the Portal?"

Mr. Tabby didn't answer. Everyone looked at Dr. Woo. She'd been sitting quietly, deep in thought. "Doctor?" Mr. Tabby said.

"Max is fully capable of flying the Portal," she said quietly. "He can do anything." Then she straightened her shoulders and narrowed her eyes. "But we are equally capable. There is an ancient Chinese warfare strategy that goes something like this—lure your enemy onto the roof, then take away the ladder."

Pearl didn't know anything about ancient Chinese warfare, but what Dr. Woo had said made sense. "If the sugar fairies came here, then Maximus couldn't get any dust," Pearl said. "And that would mean he'd be stuck in the Imaginary World, like someone on a roof with no ladder."

"That's a great idea," Ben said. "If Maximus can't travel to the Known World, then he can't sell anything. Then there's no reason for him to take any horns or hurt any creatures."

Twanabeth rose into the air, her wings beating frantically. "Dr. Woo, is it true? The fairies will be safe with you?"

"Yes, they will be safe," Dr. Woo said. "But it will be a temporary visit. Ultimately, we must figure out how to get Max out of the Imaginary World once and for all."

Mr. Tabby opened the office door. "It seems we will be having houseguests," he said. "I shall prepare the fifth floor. When will they be arriving?"

At that moment, a gruff voice shot out of a speaker that was set into the wall. "Emergency code red, emergency code reeeeed." The voice belonged to Vinny, the satyr who worked the night shift on the tenth floor. "We got an unauthorized Portal arrival, folks." The office trembled and items on the shelves rattled as the Portal touched down on the tenth floor. "Uh-oh," Vinny said. "What are you doing here? Hey, you can't do that! You can't go outside! Come baaaaack!"

"What's going on up there?" Pearl asked.

"Look!" Ben cried, pointing out the window.

It was well past midnight. Outside, the sky was still dark and cloudless. But as Pearl gazed out Dr. Woo's window, a little cloud appeared. A cloud made, not of water molecules, but of tiny flying creatures.

"They're here! They're here!" Twanabeth sang. Then she flew through a crack in the window and joined her swarm.

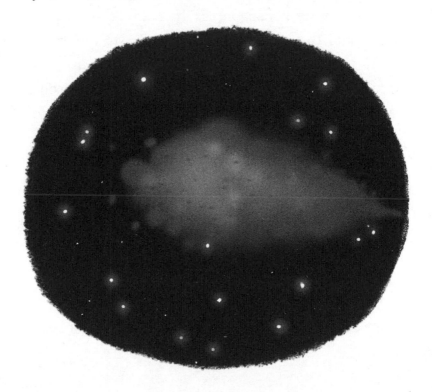

9

FURRY HANDS

Where are they going?" Ben asked as the fairy swarm flew beyond Button Lake, toward the surrounding forest.

"To make mischief," Mr. Tabby replied.

Pearl watched as the swarm tightened into a writhing ball, then dove into the trees. "At least they didn't head to town," she said. "That would be a disaster."

"My dear girl, it is only a matter of time before the sugar fairies realize that a Known World forest is nothing like an Imaginary World forest. The trees around here are not made of spun sugar. There are no teacup flowers filled with butterscotch syrup, nor do sprinkles rain from the sky. As soon as they get hungry, they will head into town in search of sweets."

Pearl thought of the syrup bottles at the diner, the cherry licorice at the movie theater, and the candy aisle at the Food 4 Less Market. Even the Dollar Store sold candy. How terrifying it would be for her parents if the swarm invaded. The wiener dogs would go ballistic!

"Mr. Tabby is correct." Dr. Woo turned away from the window. "Though the fairies have come here seeking protection, we can't have them flying free. Even without magic, they will wreak havoc on your town. Until we figure out how to get Max out of the Imaginary World once and for all, Twanabeth and her sugar fairies will need to stay in the hospital, where we can keep an eye on them." She grabbed her coffee mug and took a big sip. Then, with a resolute expression, she said, "They must be caught, right away."

"How will we catch them?" Ben asked.

"We have one thing working in our favor." A strand

of long hair fell across the doctor's face. She pushed it aside. "Sugar fairies aren't nocturnal. They will most likely nest in the trees for the night. But once the sun rises, there will be trouble."

"So that means we need to catch them before sunrise," Pearl said.

"We're going into the forest?" Ben asked with a gulp. "In the dark? Do you think that's safe?" He shuffled nervously. "Aren't there wolves? Or bears?"

"Don't be silly," Pearl told him. "Wolves are just overgrown dogs. And we haven't seen a bear around here since last summer. Or maybe it was this summer. I can't remember. But it was just a grizzly."

"Those are the worst!" Ben exclaimed.

Mr. Tabby picked up his creature calculator and typed on its little keyboard. "A grizzly bear rates a five on the danger scale, but that is only if you wander into its territory or threaten its cubs." Ben didn't look relieved. Five was the highest rating.

Dr. Woo didn't flinch at the mention of a grizzly. She'd clearly dealt with much more dangerous creatures. She looked calmly at Ben. "Neither you nor

Pearl is expected to venture into the forest against your will. But I could certainly use your help."

Ben rubbed the back of his neck. "Uh, what do sugar fairies rate on the danger scale?"

"With magic, they rate a five. Without magic, they rate a two," Mr. Tabby said. "Their mischief will result in theft and vandalism, mostly. And, as you now know, they bite if provoked."

The pain hadn't been as bad as an actual bee sting. If it meant saving the Imaginary World, Pearl could handle a few more bites if necessary. "I'll do it!" she said. Then, despite her excitement, she yawned. And, because yawns tend to be infectious, Ben yawned, too.

"This may turn into an all-nighter," Dr. Woo warned.

"No problem," Pearl said. Though she'd never had any luck staying awake all night, she wouldn't miss this opportunity, even if she had to tape her eyelids open. "My parents know I'm here, so they won't worry about me. And Ben left a note for his grandpa." Ben nodded. "So how do we catch them?

With this?" She picked up the butterfly net that Dr. Woo had used to catch Twanabeth.

"I have something better in mind. Follow me." Dr. Woo led them into the hallway and stopped at the elevator. It was already there, waiting. "I want you and Ben to bring the sasquatch to the fifth-floor Fairy Lounge. We'll meet you there."

"The sasquatch?" they both asked.

"Yes, we'll need help collecting the fairies and containing them."

"But that means the sasquatch will be going into the woods, and I thought creatures weren't supposed to leave the hospital," Ben said. The last time the sasquatch had gotten loose, it had caused a lot of trouble at the senior center.

"Under normal circumstances that is correct, but this is a dire situation. We need as many hands as we can get, even if they are furry." She and Mr. Tabby waited while Pearl and Ben stepped into the elevator. Then Dr. Woo reached in and pushed the third-floor button. "See you soon," she said.

Just before the doors closed completely, Pearl

overheard Dr. Woo say to Mr. Tabby, "I fear my time here is nearing an end. We must…" As the elevator ascended, Dr. Woo's voice faded away.

"Huh?" Pearl turned to Ben. "Did you hear that? What does she mean, her time here is nearing an end? Is she going to move? I don't want her to move." Pearl felt panicky, but Ben yawned again. His eyelids closed halfway. "Don't you care about Dr. Woo moving?"

"Sure I care. I'm just so tired." He wobbled a bit.

She grabbed his shoulders and shook him. "Don't fall asleep. This could be the most important day of our apprenticeship ever."

"You mean *night*," he corrected. The elevator stopped and the doors opened.

Each time they stepped into the Forest Suite, Pearl was amazed. The entire third floor had been turned into a natural habitat for forest-dwelling creatures. A little stream ran through the center, curling past trees that grew to the ceiling. Dew dripped from branches, mushrooms sprouted from moss, and somewhere in the depths, a tree frog croaked its hellos. A row of windows on the far wall revealed the starless night sky.

"Here, sasquatchy," Pearl called as she pushed past some ferns. It didn't have a name other than Sasquatch. In fact, they didn't even know if it was a boy or a girl. "Here, sasquatchy!"

"I bet it's sleeping," Ben said. Mist swirled around his head. He buttoned his pajama top all the way to his chin.

They'd visited the Forest Suite many times in bright daylight—to give the sasquatch a flea bath, to trim its nails, to do yoga—but Pearl had never noticed a cave, a nest, or a regular sort of a bed.

"Where do sasquatches sleep?" she wondered.

"Maybe there's a light switch," Ben said. He felt around the wall. "Oh, here it is." He and Pearl squinted as light instantly flooded the room. "Yikes, that's bright." Then a growl pierced the air, followed by cracking branches and thundering footsteps. "Uh-oh."

"There's nothing to worry about," Pearl assured Ben. The sasquatch had proven, time and time again, that it was not to be feared. It was a chocolate-loving, goofy sort of creature.

"But it sounds mad. I woke it up. I hate being woken up. Especially if I'm in the middle of a nice dream."

He had a point. The sasquatch was seven feet four inches tall and strong enough to pick each of them up with one hand. The growling grew louder. Pearl began to feel a little shaky.

A couple of frogs leaped out of the way as the sasquatch stomped over a huckleberry bush. When Pearl saw the creature, she stopped worrying and giggled. It was wearing a nightcap and holding a teddy bear. And it had a terrible case of bedhead all over its furry body. The sasquatch stood in front of them, opened its mouth, and growled again.

"We're sorry we woke you up," Pearl said, "but Dr. Woo needs your help." The sasquatch closed its mouth, took off its nightcap, then scratched its brown nose.

"Yeah," Ben said. "We're supposed to meet her on the fifth floor." He stepped into the elevator. "Come on," he motioned. But the creature wouldn't budge. Ben tried taking its hand and pulling. Pearl tried pushing. But it wasn't easy to move four hundred and ten pounds of fur. "Do you have any chocolate?" Ben asked. "Or gum?"

Pearl almost always had gum on her, and she and Ben had learned that the best way to motivate the sasquatch was through its stomach. "I'm in my pajamas. I don't have—" She reached into the pocket of her pajama pants and pulled out a pack of Fruity Chews. "Oh, I guess I do."

The sasquatch dropped the teddy bear and tried to grab the pack. Pearl stepped back.

"Oh no, you don't. I'm not picking this out of your fur again." The creature grunted, pointing to its mouth. "Okay, just one piece. But only if you come with us."

As she backed into the elevator, Pearl waved the gum. After the sasquatch had lumbered inside, she handed it a single piece. Ben quickly pushed 5. As the elevator made its ascent, the sasquatch happily chewed, wrapper and all. It took another piece to get the creature out of the elevator, but so far, so good. They'd followed Dr. Woo's instructions.

The fifth-floor hallway looked much like the hospital's other hallways, with dim lighting and lots of closed doors. Pearl and Ben glanced up and down, wondering where they were supposed to go. While Pearl held the sasquatch's hand, Ben began to wander, trying the doorknobs to see if any would open. "Here it is," he called upon reaching the last door.

"Come on," Pearl told the sasquatch. She was excited to see the fairies' special room, but Dr. Woo's words still rang in her mind.

I fear my time here is nearing an end.

The sign on the door read, FIRST CLASS FAIRY LOUNGE. Below the sign, in the center of the door, a tiny door had been built. And it had a tiny doorknob.

Ben's knuckle was too big for the fairy-sized door, so he knocked on the bigger one. No answer. "Did Dr. Woo tell us to meet her inside?"

"I think so," Pearl said. Ben turned the knob.

And what they found was a wonder to behold.

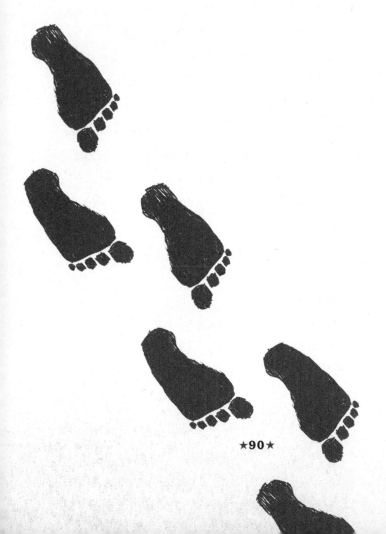

10

THE FIRST CLASS FAIRY LOUNGE

The room looked like an old-fashioned candy store, the kind Pearl wished would open in Buttonville. Floor-to-ceiling shelves held dozens of clear bowls filled with different confections. Marshmallows, peanut brittle, and white chocolate kisses caught Pearl's eye. There were jelly beans in every color and flavor. The jars were labeled LEMON DROP, TANGERINE, PINEAPPLE, GUAVA, SUGARPLUM, and KIWI, to name a few. A cotton candy machine stood in one corner, a caramel corn machine in the other. But the most beautiful thing in the room was the stone unicorn fountain that spouted rainbow sprinkles from its horn.

"Wow," Pearl said as she walked across the black-and-white-checkered floor. "Look at this." She pointed to a tree growing in the center of the room. It looked ordinary, but upon closer inspection, she saw that its leaves were actually shaped like tiny chairs, tables, sofas, and beds. "Fairy furniture."

Ben's stomach growled. "Do you think we can eat some of this stuff while we're waiting for Dr. Woo?"

Pearl shrugged. "I don't see why not. There's no sign saying it's against the rules. Besides, we can't catch a whole swarm of fairies on an empty stomach." The sasquatch was already enjoying a bowl of dark chocolate truffles. It made happy grunting sounds as it ate handfuls. Pearl tried to grab one of the truffles, but the sasquatch growled at her. "Hey, I always share my gum with you."

Its eyes widened, as if considering her comment. Then, after a shrug, it pulled a truffle out of its left nostril and handed it to her.

"Uh, thanks?" she said.

"I wouldn't eat that if I were you," Ben told her.

Pearl rolled her eyes. "Of course I'm not going to eat it," she whispered to him. "I'm just trying to be polite." When the sasquatch wasn't looking, she quickly dropped the gooey truffle into a garbage can that was filled with candy wrappers. Then she pointed to the top shelf. "But I'd sure like a few peanut butter cups."

Ben climbed onto a stepladder and reached into a bowl. He tossed a few of the foil-covered cups to Pearl, then took some gumdrops for himself. "Sugar fairies are so lucky. My mom never lets me eat candy," he said with a huge grin.

"My dad says sugar makes me hyper," Pearl said. "I don't think that's true. I'm *always* hyper." She ate three peanut butter cups, then reached into a jar of papaya-flavored jelly beans.

"Attention, please." Mr. Tabby stood in the doorway, wearing his usual serious expression. He was holding a big plastic container.

Pearl dropped the beans. Would they get a stern

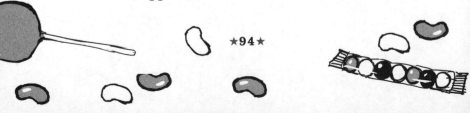

lecture from Mr. Tabby and then be assigned some sort of punishment, like cleaning earwax from the sasquatch's ears or flossing its teeth? "Did we break a rule?" she asked, ready to defend her actions. After all, how could they be expected to work all night without some sort of food?

"Not that I am aware of. But as past behavior predicts future behavior, I expect you will break a rule or two before the night is through." He strode into the room and removed the truffle bowl from the sasquatch's chocolate-covered hands.

Ben jumped off the stepladder. "Where's Dr. Woo?"

"Dr. Woo is answering a telephone call from the Imaginary World."

"What's wrong?" Pearl asked. "Is the call about Maximus Steele? Did he do something bad?"

"Did he hurt another creature?"

Mr. Tabby didn't respond. Pearl fidgeted. It drove her nuts when Mr. Tabby ignored their questions. "Why would he hurt another creature?" she asked. "There's no way for him to sell horns if he can't travel through the Portal."

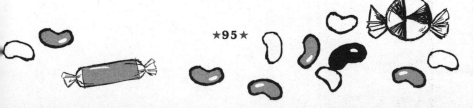

"Right," Ben said. "He's stuck on a roof with no ladder, just like Dr. Woo planned."

"Indeed." Mr. Tabby glanced away, which made Pearl sense that he was hiding something. Then he smoothed his vest, the way he often did before launching into a series of instructions. "Now, listen very carefully. Tonight you will venture into the forest beyond Button Lake and catch as many fairies as you can. Sugar will serve as your bait." He opened the container that he'd brought into the Fairy Lounge. It was the size and shape of a barrel. He filled the bottom of the container with kiwi-flavored jelly beans, then closed the lid. "This is a special trap, designed by Dr. Woo. If you shake the trap, the kiwi scent will be released through microscopic pores. The fairies will fly in through this one-way chute. They will be distracted by the jelly beans, and by the time they realize they can't get out, you will be carrying them back to the hospital." Mr. Tabby handed the trap to Ben, who could barely fit his arms around it.

"What if they bite us?" Ben asked.

"It is highly likely that they will. Fairies are notoriously temperamental. Are you allergic to fairy bites?"

"Obviously *I'm* not," Pearl said, pointing to her earlobe, which felt totally normal again.

"Uh, I don't know," Ben said with a shrug. "I'm allergic to other things."

"Well, if after a fairy bite your eyeballs get itchy, then return to the hospital immediately for a fairy antivenom shot."

"I hate shots," Ben grumbled.

"Me too, but itchy eyeballs sound way worse," Pearl told him.

The sasquatch had grabbed a bowl of milk chocolate coins and wasn't bothering to remove the gold foil. Mr. Tabby swiftly took the bowl from him. "That is quite enough. It is time to get to work." He led the sasquatch into the hallway, with Pearl and Ben right behind.

"Why is the sasquatch coming with us?" Ben

asked, waddling as he carried the trap.

"In case there are forest predators, the sasquatch will protect you."

Pearl thought this was a great idea. While she knew the sasquatch was nice, a bear wouldn't know that. But she also knew the sasquatch got distracted easily. Would it actually protect them? "What about Metalmouth? Couldn't he come with us?"

"Metalmouth is..." Again, Mr. Tabby looked away. What was he hiding? "He is engaged in an important activity at the moment." The words *important activity* sent a new list of questions straight to Pearl's tongue, but she knew Mr. Tabby wouldn't provide any answers. And she didn't want to further annoy him. His mustache was twitching something fierce already.

"Can the sasquatch carry this thing?" Ben asked. "It's pretty heavy."

"Under no circumstances are you to hand the trap to the sasquatch," Mr. Tabby said. "It would eat all the jelly beans."

Pearl couldn't help herself. One question popped
out. "Hey, Mr. Tabby, is the sasquatch a boy or a
girl? I mean, I can't tell." Pearl patted its arm. "No
offense," she told it. The sasquatch picked a piece
of gold foil from its teeth and grunted.

"The sasquatch does not have a gender."

"Really?" Pearl frowned. "Uh, what does that mean?"

"It is neither a he nor a she. It is simply what it is." He took a ring of keys from his pocket and locked the tiny fairy door with a tiny key. "After you catch the sugar fairies, release them inside the lounge. Then close the big door. They will not be able to escape." He folded his arms behind his back and looked down at them. "Do you understand your instructions?" Pearl and Ben nodded. The sasquatch didn't nod. It just scratched its bum.

Pearl helped Ben carry the trap into the elevator and through the downstairs lobby. Mr. Tabby slid the five dead bolts and opened the front door.

"Mr. Tabby?" This time, Ben was doing the asking. "Metalmouth said that you'd just returned from a quest. What kind of quest?"

"That is none of your concern." Mr. Tabby ushered Pearl and Ben outside.

"If Dr. Woo's still talking on the phone, then that's a pretty long conversation," Pearl pointed out,

hoping Mr. Tabby might give them a clue as to what was going on. But he didn't take the bait.

"Make your way quickly," he told them. "It would be regrettable if something were to happen to you." Was that a look of concern in his yellow eyes? "Be careful."

"*Careful* is basically my middle name," Ben said.

The hospital door shut, leaving Pearl, Ben, and the sasquatch on the front steps. A lone howl rose in the distance. The sasquatch whimpered and stepped behind Pearl.

And darkness closed in.

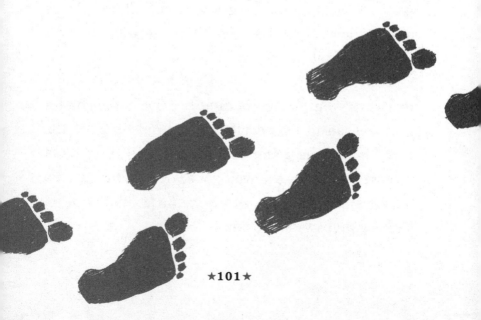

11

SHOOTING SUGAR STARS

I can't see more than three feet in front of me," Pearl complained.

"Maybe that's a good thing," Ben said as another howl filled the air. "Then we won't be able to see the wolf when it eats us."

Pearl knew he was kidding, but with the sasquatch trying to hide behind her back, Ben had a good reason to be worried. It didn't look as if the furry giant was going to offer much in the way of protection, unless the wolf got scared off by the sasquatch's *unique* odor, which was a combination of wet dog and sweaty socks.

"I know what to do." Ben set down the trap, then rolled up his pajama sleeve and pressed a button on his fancy gold watch. "It has a flashlight function," he explained as the watch lit up. He pointed it at the sasquatch's face. "This works great." The sasquatch growled. "Oops, sorry." He aimed the beam lower.

Because Ben was wearing their only source of light, Pearl offered to carry the trap so that Ben could lead the way around the hospital to Button Lake. But Pearl didn't like walking in the middle.

Ben's pace was too slow, and the sasquatch kept stepping on her heels.

"Hey, stop pushing," Ben said. "I'm going as fast as I can. This would be so much easier if we had a full moon."

"If we had a full moon, that wolf might turn into a werewolf," Pearl said.

Ben snorted. "That's ridiculous. Werewolves aren't real."

"Uh, hello? We're walking with a *sasquatch*, and you're telling me werewolves aren't real."

Ben stopped in his tracks. He whipped around. "You're right. Werewolves *could* be real." The watch light shone up his nostrils, casting dark, eerie circles beneath his eyes. He lowered his voice to a whisper. "What if we run into one?"

"Dr. Woo would never send us into that kind of danger," Pearl assured him.

"Sure she would," Ben said. "She had me feed a fish to that kid-eating kelpie, remember?"

How could Pearl forget that moment? But even so, Ben always got a bit scared when they were

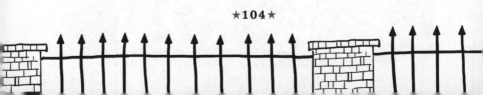

about to do something new. The trap was slipping between her arms, so with a grunt, she heaved it higher. "Come on. Let's keep walking."

A narrow trail hugged the edge of the lake, then turned toward the forest. Apparently the sasquatch wasn't fond of the dark, because it held tight to the back of Pearl's pajama top. Mrs. Petal would have given Pearl a reprimand for walking at night without a jacket, but thankfully, the night air wasn't chilly. And her leprechaun shoes kept her feet snug and warm. "I'm still wondering what Dr. Woo meant when she said her time here might be nearing an end. Do you think she's going to leave Buttonville? Why wouldn't Mr. Tabby tell us what Metalmouth is doing? And who do you think Dr. Woo is talking to?"

"I don't know." Ben stopped walking. They'd reached the wrought-iron fence that enclosed the old button factory property. A wide section was missing. Ben aimed his watch at the ground. "Tire tracks," he said. "And they look fresh." While Pearl peered over Ben's shoulder, the sasquatch tried to snatch the fairy trap.

"Oh no, you don't. This is not for you," she told it, feeling a bit like a mother scolding her child. The sasquatch grunted. Ben nearly jumped out of his shoes.

"*What* was that?" he cried.

"Just the sasquatch," Pearl said calmly. "Keep going."

Ben took extra-slow steps as he led them into the forest. In a short time, they found themselves standing in a clearing, surrounded by towering pine trees. "Maybe this would be a good place to try the trap," he said. Pearl was happy to set it down and give her aching arms a rest. But as she did, a bright light flicked on.

Ben and Pearl gasped. The sasquatch ducked behind a tree.

"Howdy, y'all!" a voice called from across the clearing. Violet, the switchboard operator, stood in the doorway of an RV, holding a lantern. "What are you little darlings doing out here in the middle of the niiiiight?" The sasquatch must have recognized her voice, because it stepped out from behind the tree and waved.

"Dr. Woo sent us," Pearl explained. "What are you doing here?"

"This is where Vinny and I live," she said with a sweep of her furry arm. Vinny was Violet's brother. They were both satyrs, which meant that they were half human, half goat. "Come on over here so I can get a better look at y'aaaaall."

Pearl was happy to see a familiar face in the

spooky forest. Violet set the lantern on a picnic table, which was covered in a pretty red-checkered cloth. A bag of oats sat on the table, along with a bag of barley and a bundle of ivy vines. "Would you like a snack?" Violet asked as she began to chew on a vine. She was dressed in a flannel nightgown and robe that had one of those fancy feathered collars. Her blond hair was wound up in curlers. "Looks like we're having ourselves a little slumber partyyyyy." Her tiny goat eyes sparkled in the lantern light. "Now, tell me, whatever is going on?"

"I found a sugar fairy," Pearl whispered, in case the little mischief-makers were hiding nearby. "She's the queen."

"*And* she's the missing apprentice, Twanabeth Twilight," Ben added.

"She flew into the woods with her swarm." Pearl leaned close to Violet. "We're supposed to catch them."

"I seeeee." Violet had reached the end of the vine, so she grabbed another. And a handful of oats. She chewed quickly, as if she hadn't eaten in days. Every

satyr Pearl and Ben had met thus far seemed to be constantly hungry.

"Are you going on a trip?" Ben pointed to some suitcases that were stacked next to the table.

Violet swallowed. "Dr. Woo said that we should…" She paused to brush stray oats from her little goat beard. "Well, I might be taking a trip, and I might not. I don't rightly knooooow."

Pearl sensed that the full truth was not being revealed. "Dr. Woo said her time here might be nearing an end. Are you guys moving?" Desperation filled her voice. "Please don't leave Buttonville. It won't be the same without you!"

"Now, now, little daaaaarling. Don't go getting yourself all discombobulated about things you can't control. Nobody is going anywhere tonight." She pulled Pearl into a big motherly hug. The feathered collar tickled Pearl's nose. "You stop your fretting." She released Pearl, then grabbed another handful of oats. "I'm glad Dr. Woo sent you out here. Those nasty fairies swooped in and ate all my honey. Then they flew up into those treeeees." She pointed above their heads. "They're up there right now, snoring as loud as June bugs. Listen." She cupped a hand around her pointed goat ear. Pearl and Ben tilted their heads. Sure enough, a faint buzzing sound drifted down from the branches.

"We'd better shake the trap and release the kiwi scent," Ben said.

"Right." Pearl went to grab it. "Oh no. Sasquatch!"

The sasquatch was sitting on the forest floor, looking as guilty as a kid with a hand in a cookie jar—except in this case it was a creature with its hand in a fairy trap. And, unfortunately, the trap was empty. "We can't take you anywhere," Pearl said with a stomp of her foot.

"Wait, it might still work," Ben said, pointing to the sasquatch's arm. Then its leg. Then its back. Dozens of green jelly beans were stuck all over its fur.

"What did it do? Dump them over its head?" Pearl asked. One was even stuck to the sasquatch's nose.

Pearl and Ben tried to pick off the sticky candies, but they clung like glue. No matter how hard

Pearl pulled, she couldn't get them untangled. The sasquatch yelped as they yanked and tugged. Then, with a frustrated groan, it scrambled to its feet and started jumping around, trying to shake the jelly beans free. As the jumping continued, the lovely, fruity scent of kiwi filled the air.

The sky suddenly lit up, as if the stars had woken and switched on their night-lights.

But they weren't stars. Pearl knew because they revved their little winged motors and flew straight at the sasquatch.

"Fairies!" Ben yelled.

The sasquatch whimpered and covered its face with its furry hands. Violet hid under the picnic table. Ben and Pearl covered their earlobes.

"Here! They! Come!" Pearl hollered above the high-pitched squealing.

The first batch of fairies dove straight at the jelly beans. But just like the candies, the fairies got tangled in the sasquatch's thick fur. And the more they writhed, trying to get free, the more tangled they became.

"Wow," Ben said. "Sasquatch fur makes a pretty good fairy trap."

After the first wave of fairies got stuck, the rest of the fairies flew away, disappearing into the dark trees.

"Drat!" Pearl exclaimed. "We didn't catch them all."

"At least we caught some of them," Ben said.

The sasquatch stopped jumping and started swatting at the buzzing creatures. "No, don't do that." Pearl grabbed one of its hands. "We don't want to hurt them." The sasquatch furrowed its sloping brow and grunted unhappily. "Well, this isn't *our* fault," Pearl told it. "You're the one who opened the trap."

"Better giddyup to the hospital," Violet said as she climbed out from under the table. "Before those fairies escape agaaaaain." She brushed pine needles off her robe, grabbed one of the suitcases and the lantern, and disappeared inside the RV.

Once again, Ben guided the way. Pearl picked up the empty trap, then walked behind the sasquatch, ready to intervene if it started swatting again. As the tangled fairies continued to glow, Pearl stifled a giggle. "You kinda look like a Christmas tree," she told the sasquatch.

Once they reached the First Class Fairy Lounge, they began to pick the fairies out of the sasquatch's fur. There was no creature calculator to help translate, but Pearl was pretty sure the fairies were saying all sorts of mean things because they were squealing and buzzing like crazy. It was slow going, and the sasquatch grew grumpier by the minute. To find all the fairies, Pearl persuaded the sasquatch to stretch into some of its favorite yoga poses. Downward-facing dog was especially helpful in reaching the fairies who were stuck to its rump. And warrior two helped locate the ones stuck in its armpit. Pearl and Ben kept a lookout for Twanabeth. "I don't think we caught her," Ben said.

Neither Mr. Tabby nor Dr. Woo showed up to help. This worried Pearl.

"Maybe that phone call turned out to be an emergency," Ben suggested. "Maybe Dr. Woo had to go to the Imaginary World."

"Yeah, but where's Mr. Tabby?" The assistant

didn't like going to the Imaginary World, because he turned into a cat the moment he stepped out of the Portal. But there was no one to answer their questions, so all they could do was keep on picking and plucking.

Finally, as the first rays of dawn appeared, the sasquatch was fairy-free. And Pearl had five bites on her right hand and two on her left, while Ben had been bitten on each finger and on both earlobes. Thankfully, neither of them came down with itchy eyeballs. And the fairies had stopped biting. Having feasted on candy, the little winged creatures were settled on the tree branches, in the lounge chairs and sofas.

"I think we're done," Ben said with a huge yawn.

"Let's go find Dr. Woo." They led the sleepy sasquatch into the hall, closed the door, and bumped right into Mr. Tabby.

"I shall escort the sasquatch back to its habitat," Mr. Tabby informed them. "And you two should check in with your families."

"We didn't catch all the fairies," Pearl said. Her

eyelids felt as heavy as wet towels. "And we didn't find Twanabeth."

"But we got some," Ben said, rubbing his eyes.

"Dr. Woo and I will attempt to capture the rest of the swarm," Mr. Tabby told them. "Go home and get some rest."

Pearl didn't have the strength for questions. She was wondering about Dr. Woo, the emergency call, and how they'd catch the rest of the fairies. She wanted to know about the quest that Dr. Woo, Mr. Tabby, and Metalmouth had gone on, and why Violet was packing. But her thoughts felt very thick, and when she opened her mouth, the only thing that came out was a yawn.

She and Ben didn't speak on the walk home. They lumbered like sasquatches. Pearl barely remembered passing the park and duck pond, barely remembered grunting a "hi" to her parents as she headed for her bedroom.

Then she landed face-first on her bed and began snoring like a June bug.

12

INVASION OF THE KILLER BEES

Pearl slept so deeply she barely moved.
But she dreamed.

Mostly of fairies—pretty little things that danced in the air and made music with their wings. They invited her to a tea party, where she sat on a gumdrop stool and ate sugar crystals from a tiny buttercup bowl. The fairies smiled sweetly at her. They offered her more sugar and put flowers in her hair. But then, just as Pearl was about to grow her own wings and start flying, the fairies began biting her all over! And they began to wail in a strange way. Wailing and biting, *wailing* and *biting*!

Pearl bolted upright, waving her arms to ward off the attacking beasts. But as the fog of sleep faded, she realized it had only been a dream. She was safe in her room. No biting.

But the wailing sound was coming from outside.

Pearl scrambled out of bed and threw back the curtains. Sunlight nearly blinded her. *It's the middle of the day*, she realized. As she opened her bedroom window, the wailing sound grew louder. She leaned out to get a better view. A police car drove down Main Street, its siren blaring, and stopped outside the Buttonville Cinema. Pearl's aunt, Officer Milly, got out of the squad car and ran into the theater. Pearl glanced at her bedside clock. 4:10 PM. The special matinee of *Invasion of the Killer Bees* would be playing.

"Pearl!" Ben stood on the sidewalk below.

"What's going on?" Pearl called down to him.

"I don't know," he yelled. "I was sleeping, and the siren woke me up."

"I'll be right down."

Ben had changed out of his pajamas, and even though Pearl didn't want to miss a moment of excitement, she grabbed a pair of basketball shorts and a T-shirt from her dresser. Why was her aunt at the movie theater? And why had her parents let her sleep so long? She had work to do. She had fairies to catch!

By the time she'd dressed and run downstairs, Mr. and Mrs. Petal were standing on the sidewalk next to Ben. They both wore their Dollar Store aprons.

"Hello, sweetie," Mrs. Petal said. "How was your nap?"

"Fine." Pearl looked down the street. Although the siren had stopped, the red light on the police car was still flashing. "What's Aunt Milly doing?"

"There's been some sort of disturbance at the cinema," Mr. Petal said. "We heard screaming."

"Maybe the movie is too scary," Mrs. Petal suggested.

The cinema's front door flung open, and Mr. Bumfrickle hobbled out, moving as fast as his

arthritic legs could carry him. "Killer bees!" he hollered, a wild look on his face.

He was followed by Maybell, a frequent visitor at the senior center. As she bounded down the stairs, she spilled her jumbo-sized tub of popcorn. "Outta my way!"

Mr. Dill and Mrs. Dill raced out the door, as did Mr. Filbert. "We've been stung!"

And then came Ben's grandfather. He raised his cane in the air and hollered, "*Oy gevalt!* We're under attack!"

"I think you're right," Mr. Petal told his wife. "That movie is definitely too scary."

Pearl pulled Ben aside. "There's a lot of sugar in a movie theater," she whispered.

He nodded. "I was thinking the same thing."

Pearl was about to suggest that they get some jelly beans, jars, and butterfly nets from the Dollar Store when she suddenly saw *red*. Victoria Mulberry and her mother, wearing their red overalls and red baseball caps, barreled out the cinema's door and pushed past the elderly patrons.

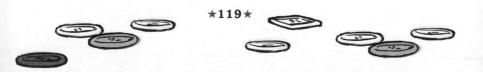

"My daughter's been stung! She's allergic to bees! Call an ambulance! Call the National Guard!" Mrs. Mulberry exclaimed. Victoria, looking a bit dazed, rubbed both earlobes.

"Uh-oh," Pearl said. Just a few weeks ago, Victoria had caught Troll Tonsillitis, and her entire head had swelled up like a balloon. If she was allergic to fairy bites, then her eyeballs would start to itch, and who knew what else might happen? Pearl and Ben would have to run and get an antivenom shot from Mr. Tabby. What a nuisance that would be!

"Mom, I'm not having a reaction," Victoria said. "I'm fine. I must not be allergic to *killer* bees."

Mrs. Mulberry examined her daughter's earlobes. "Well, I still think we should call for help. This could be a matter of national security. Does anyone have the telephone number for the president?"

While Victoria and her mother argued about what should be done and who should be called, Pearl nudged Ben with her elbow. "Let's go see if we can find the fairies," she said.

"Okay."

"Sweetie, I don't want you watching that movie!" Mrs. Petal called as Pearl and Ben dashed across the street. "It will give you nightmares!" But they didn't stop running. They passed Grandpa Abe. They passed Maybell and Mr. Bumfrickle. They didn't even glance at the Mulberrys as they bounded up the stairs and into the cinema.

"Pearl, Ben, stay back!" Officer Milly leaped in front of the kids, blocking them with her arms. "It's too dangerous in here. Get outside!"

Pearl peered over and under her aunt's arm,

trying to get a full view of the lobby. Ms. Wartwell, who sold the movie tickets and refreshments, was cowering behind the popcorn machine. Shredded candy boxes lay on the floor and all over the counter, as if they'd been torn by a hundred tiny hands and teeth. Which, as Pearl and Ben knew, was exactly what had happened.

"Help," Ms. Wartwell said in a small, timid voice. "The killer bees are going to eat me. Help me, please." She pointed to a churning cloud that was attacking a box of caramel corn.

"Don't worry, Marilyn. We'll get you out of here," Officer Milly told her. "Walk slowly toward me." But Ms. Wartwell wouldn't budge. "You can do it. Walk over here, to the door. Come on." It was like trying to coax a cat into a bathtub. Ms. Wartwell wasn't going anywhere.

Pearl wasn't worried about Ms. Wartwell. The fairies wouldn't eat her. But they sure had made a mess. And now that the police department was involved, catching the fairies *in secret* was going to be difficult. The swarm, having finished the

caramel corn, swooped round and round, high-pitched whining bouncing off the lobby walls.

"Twanabeth," Pearl called. "Twanabeth, stop doing this. You're scaring everyone!"

"Who's Twanabeth?" Officer Milly asked. Then she yelled, "Duck!"

With a swoosh, the swarm flew over their heads and out the lobby door. Pearl and Ben turned on their heels and ran outside.

In a matter of minutes, Buttonville had transformed from a sleepy little town into a hub of chaos. Such mayhem hadn't been seen in the town since the great water main break of '79, when the streets had flooded so quickly people had to swim to safety.

Onlookers screamed and pointed to the humming swarm. A car honked. Another crashed into a streetlamp. The fairies flew through the diner's open window. More screaming arose as Lucy and Lionel rushed out.

"Help!" they both cried. The gathering crowd watched through the picture windows as the fairies

turned bottles upside down and poured syrup all over the counter. The syrup was lapped up almost instantaneously, and the swarm was on the move again, heading into the Food 4 Less Market.

The Food 4 Less cashier ran out. "Help, *help*! There are bugs in the store!" Pearl and Ben ran to the window, and, sure enough, the fairies were tearing into bags of brown sugar.

"Unbelievable!" Ben said. "How much sugar can those things eat?"

"What are we going to do?" Pearl asked. "This is terrible!"

"Attention, everyone!" Officer Milly stood on the roof of her squad car, a megaphone in her hand. *"Attention!"* People stopped screaming and turned to listen. "It's important that we don't panic. Clearly we've been invaded by some sort of insect. We don't know what kind, exactly, or why—"

"They followed their queen," Ms. Bee said. She stepped out of the crowd. "Yesterday morning, the queen bee was inside the diner. Pearl Petal caught her. I advised Pearl to get rid of her. But if she didn't,

and if the queen has begun to nest, then that would explain why the swarm has arrived."

"I knew Pearl had something to do with this," Mrs. Mulberry said. "Why else would we have a swarm of killer bees on the loose in Buttonville? Pearl is always causing trouble!"

"Pearl?" Officer Milly looked around. "Where are you?"

Pearl gulped. The crowd parted down the middle, making room for her. She walked up to the squad car. From the squinty glares being cast her way, she knew she'd already been judged guilty as charged.

Her aunt peered over the top of her dark glasses. "Pearl, is this true?"

"It's true," Victoria said. In her usual tattle-telling way, Victoria was more than happy to provide information regarding Pearl's activities. "She told me that she'd caught a queen killer bee. She even showed it to me."

"Did you get rid of it?" Ms. Bee asked.

Pearl looked around for Ben. She could certainly use one of his stories right about now. But the crowd had squeezed closer, and she couldn't see him. At that moment, she felt very alone. She'd faced lots of complicated situations during the last month, but Ben had always been there for her. "I didn't *get rid* of it, exactly. I...I..."

The squad car began to rock back and forth as Mrs. Mulberry heaved herself onto the trunk, then climbed onto the roof. She grabbed the megaphone from Officer Milly's hand. "Have no fear, fellow Buttonvillers. As the president of the Welcome Wagon Committee, I take the safety of our citizens as my top priority. While Pearl has brought trouble, yet again, to our peaceful town, the Mulberrys are here to save the day." She pointed at Victoria, who held up a piece of paper. "My daughter found a flyer for an exterminator. We called them and they're on the way!"

"Exterminator?" Pearl cried.

13

SHELTER FOR A DOLLAR

Pearl grabbed the flyer from Victoria's hand.

BYE-BYE, BUGS

Are creepy-crawlies bugging you?
Our aerodynamically designed Vacuumator
will suck those biting beasts right out of your
bed, hair, and house forever.
CALL 1-555-BUG-GUYS

Ben ran to her side, his cheeks red from pushing his way through the crowd. "What is it?"

"It's just like the flyer we found at the hospital," Pearl said, waving it frantically in his face. "They're on the way!"

"Here?" Ben asked.

"Someone has to clean up the mess Pearl has made." Mrs. Mulberry smiled proudly. "The exterminators will exterminate those vicious little beasts, and Buttonville will once again be a killer bee–free town."

"But they're not killer bees," Pearl insisted. She wanted to grab that megaphone and talk some sense into everyone. "I know I told Victoria that I'd caught a killer bee, but that wasn't the whole truth. They're just...regular bees. And they're not going to hurt anyone. Well, they might bite, but it's only a problem if you're allergic and..." She looked pleadingly at Ben, hoping he'd step in. Ben opened his mouth, ready to come up with some sort of brilliant story, but Mrs. Mulberry wasn't going to let him put a damper on her moment of importance. She loved being the center of attention.

With the megaphone pressed to her mouth, Mrs. Mulberry said, "Never mind your excuses, Pearl. Those bugs are out of control, and we aren't safe until they're caught and *destroyed*." The crowd murmured in agreement.

While Officer Milly began wrestling Mrs. Mulberry for possession of the megaphone, Victoria sneered at Pearl. "You're lucky I'm not allergic to killer bees, or my mom would sue you, for sure."

Pearl sneered back. Then, through clenched teeth, she said, "I wish you'd turn into a kiwi jelly bean. And then *you'd* be sorry."

"What's that supposed to mean?" Victoria asked. But there was no time for an explanation, or for Pearl to imagine Victoria as a big, fat piece of edible candy, because once again, screaming filled the air. The swarm had flown from the Food 4 Less Market and was now circling the Town Hall's clock tower. Then it dove down the Town Hall chimney.

"Keep calm, keep calm," Officer Milly said as she

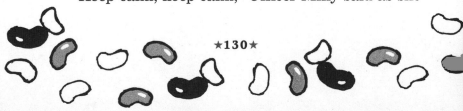

yanked the megaphone from Mrs. Mulberry's grabby hands. "Until the exterminator arrives, I'm ordering everyone to seek shelter at home. Close your windows and doors, and stay put until you hear the Town Hall bell. That will be the signal that it's safe to come out." The crowd began to disperse.

"We can't go home," Ben told Pearl. "We have to catch the fairies before the exterminator gets them!"

"If we could just find Twanabeth—" But Pearl wasn't able to finish her thought, because her father had wrapped an arm around her shoulder and was leading her up the street.

"Come along, sweetie," he told her, tightening his grip. "We need to get inside, where it's safe."

Grandpa Abe was standing next to Mrs. Petal. He waved his cane. "Ben! Hurry!"

"But, Dad, Ben and I have to do something," Pearl protested, trying to halt his progress by locking her knees.

"You and Ben can *do something* later," Mr. Petal said, steering her into the Dollar Store. "This is a very serious situation, and we all need to get off

the street before the killer bees attack again." Then he turned to Grandpa Abe. "Come in. You'll be safe with us."

Pearl stomped her foot. "But we can't be locked in the store. We have to—"

Mrs. Petal shook a finger at her daughter. "Don't argue with your father. These aren't *honey*bees. They are killers."

Pearl groaned with frustration. If she hadn't signed that contract of secrecy, she could tell them the truth. Then everyone would stop freaking out and allow her and Ben to do their jobs!

Mrs. Petal turned the Dollar Store sign to CLOSED and was about to shut the door when Mrs. Mulberry and Victoria barged in. "Well, why are you just standing there?" Mrs. Mulberry complained. "Lock that door before those beasts bite my daughter again!"

Mrs. Petal, who was always very polite, hesitated for a moment. She'd had enough run-ins with the Mulberrys to know that being locked in the store with them would most likely be an unpleasant experience. "Uh, wouldn't you be more comfortable in *your* home?" she said, managing a sweet smile.

"It's too dangerous to walk all the way home," Mrs. Mulberry said. "Besides, it's my duty to keep watch, in case anything needs to be reported to the authorities." She grabbed a pair of plastic binoculars from a bin and stepped into the display window. She didn't seem to care that it had taken the Petals half a day to create the lovely display. After pushing aside the picnic baskets, plastic dishes, and barbecue tongs, she plopped onto a picnic bench and proceeded to watch Main Street. "And it's your duty to control your troublemaking daughter."

"I'm so sick of being called a troublemaker," Pearl whispered to Ben.

With a sigh, Mrs. Petal closed the front door. Pearl clenched her fists with frustration. It was bad enough that the fairies were in danger of extermination, but now she and Ben were locked in a store with Victoria. If only that Vacuumator would work on a person!

"I'll make some tea," Mrs. Petal said, and she went upstairs to set the kettle on the stove.

"I take mine with three lumps of sugar!" Mrs. Mulberry called. Then she shrieked. "There they are! They've left Town Hall and are flying down Main Street!"

While Victoria, Grandpa Abe, and Mr. Petal rushed to the window to watch the fairies, Pearl pulled Ben down aisle two. They huddled in front of a stack of canned cheese spread. "I don't care if

I get grounded for a million years," she whispered. "We have to get out of here and find Twanabeth. We have to warn her."

"How?" Ben asked. "Mrs. Mulberry is watching *everything*. And your dad is guarding the front door."

"I saw that dragon again." Victoria had followed them down the aisle. She took off her glasses, wiped the thick lenses on her shirt, then stuck them back onto her nose. "And don't try to tell me that I didn't, because I did. It flew right over my yard."

"Go away, Victoria. Ben and I are having a *private* conversation."

"About what?"

"That's none of your beeswax." Pearl felt a bit prickly. Maybe she was allergic to Victoria. That girl got under Pearl's skin like stinging nettles! "And for the last time, dragons aren't real."

"I saw it. And I saw both of you on its back." She smirked.

Ben pointed at Victoria's glasses. "Have you had your prescription checked? Because you're obviously seeing things. Or maybe you're going mental."

Victoria stuck out her lower lip. "I'm not mental. That's a mean thing to say."

"Why can't you figure it out?" Pearl said, clenching her teeth again. "We don't want to talk to you. We *never* want to talk to you. *Go. Away.*"

Victoria winced as if those words had stung. For a millisecond, Pearl felt bad. She didn't want to hurt anyone's feelings. But then she reminded herself that there were hundreds of tiny lives at stake and, thus, no time to feel bad. Besides, Victoria constantly said mean things to Pearl. It was part of her daily routine.

"Victoria!" Mrs. Mulberry called from the display window. "I've had a brilliant idea. I'm going to write about our situation for the upcoming issue of *Welcome Wagon Monthly*. Get some paper and a pen."

"Better do what your mom says," Pearl told her. "Paper and pens are in aisle one."

"Thank you, Mrs. Mulberry," Ben whispered as Victoria went to get the supplies. And while he and Pearl continued to huddle next to the cheese spread, trying to hatch a plan, Mrs. Mulberry dictated to her daughter, who'd joined her in the front window.

"It was a dark and stormy day when we found ourselves trapped," Mrs. Mulberry began, her voice filled with drama. "The Dollar Store, a wasteland of useless objects, had become our only shelter from an invading army of vicious insects that were determined to prey on our flesh. With no food or water to sustain us, Victoria and I grew weak. But I was determined to keep us alive!"

"Impressive," Ben said. "Sounds like one of my stories."

Pearl rolled her eyes. "We need to get out of here. What are we going to do?"

"Tea is ready!" Mrs. Petal called from the upstairs apartment.

"You got a little something to nosh?" Grandpa Abe asked. "All this excitement's made me hungry."

"Sure," Mr. Petal told him. Then he led Grandpa Abe up the stairs.

"I can't leave my post," Mrs. Mulberry announced. "Victoria, dear, bring Mummy a cup of tea." Victoria set the paper and pen aside and followed Grandpa Abe and Mr. Petal. Pearl took a deep, focused breath. With everyone upstairs and Mrs. Mulberry staring out the window, it was now or never.

"Come on," she whispered. She hurried to the back of the store, opened the basement door, and, with Ben at her heels, quickly descended into Great-Aunt Gladys's apartment.

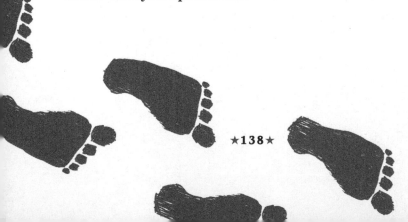

14

GHOST TOWN

It was warm in the basement, the air thick with the scent of mentholated arthritis rub and wiener dog. Gladys certainly didn't appear to be worried about killer bees. She was fast asleep in her armchair, knitting needles on her lap. Sweetness and Light were asleep, too, curled beneath knitted blankets on the couch. There was so much snoring going on that it was possible none of them had heard the police siren or the screams for help.

Because this was a basement apartment, the windows were set high in the walls. Pearl climbed onto a chair and pushed one of them open. Then she and Ben climbed out. The dogs didn't stir, nor did Aunt Gladys. Pearl quietly closed the window.

"Mrs. Mulberry said the swarm headed down Main Street. Let's go."

In order to stay out of Mrs. Mulberry's line of vision, Pearl and Ben darted behind the Dollar Store. Then they crossed Cherry Street, cut through the park, and hurried down Fir Street. Nearly out of breath, they peered around the corner of the bookstore.

There was no sign of the swarm up or down Main Street. In fact, there was no sign of anything. The crowd was gone. The police car was gone. The door to the Buttonville Cinema stood wide open, as did the diner's door. The only sign of life was a flock of pigeons enjoying Maybell's spilled popcorn. "It looks like a ghost town," Pearl said as an empty soda cup rolled down the street.

Ben wiped nervous sweat from his forehead. "Maybe the fairies got enough sugar and went back to the hospital."

"Maybe..." Pearl narrowed her eyes. "What's that?" A whining sound had arisen in the distance. She smiled. "Is it—?"

"Yeah, it's the fairies," Ben said, his eyes widening.

That high-pitched hum was definitely the swarm, but where was it coming from? Pearl and Ben turned in slow circles, scanning the nearby rooftops, the trees, the sky. But as they searched, another sound arose—a rhythmic chugging—and it came from the entrance to town, where Main Street joined the highway.

Keeping well out of view, Pearl and Ben ran toward the sound. They stopped at a sign.

WELCOME TO
·BUTTONVILLE·
"THE NICEST TOWN ON EARTH"

The chugging grew louder. "What is it?" Pearl said, looking toward the highway.

Ben poked her shoulder. "It's Victoria."

"Don't be silly. Victoria's rude and annoying, but she doesn't sound like an engine."

"No, I mean, Victoria is *right behind us*."

Pearl whipped around. Victoria's frizzy pigtails bounced as she rushed toward them. Pearl was so furious her face went as red as Victoria's overalls. "*What* are you doing?"

Victoria skidded to a stop. "How come you're out here? Officer Milly said we couldn't go outside until the Town Hall bell rang." She put her hands on her hips. "Are you going to meet the dragon? I want to meet it, too."

"We're not meeting a dragon," Ben insisted. "We're out here because..." He paused for a moment, gathering a story. "We're out here because I lost my inhaler, which I need in case I have an asthma attack. Asthma attacks can be very serious, and they can be brought on by stress. And this whole killer bee thing is very stressful. So I'm sure Officer Milly would give us permission to search for it. That's why we're out here."

"I didn't know you used an inhaler," Pearl whispered in his ear.

"I don't," he whispered back. Pearl sighed with relief, happy that they didn't have to add an asthma attack to their growing list of things to worry about.

"Go away before you get in trouble," Pearl said.

Victoria leaned against the welcome sign and folded her arms super tight. "I'm not moving, and you can't make me. I want to meet the dragon."

"Oh yeah?" Pearl took a step toward her. What was she going to do? Pick her up and carry her? Why was Victoria always getting in the way? Why did she have to be such a pest? They stared at each other, steely-eyed. It was like an old western movie, where the bad guy and the good guy got ready to draw weapons. Except this was Buttonville, and the only weapon Pearl had was words. Anger welled and spewed out like a volcano. *"I hate you!"*

Three small words, when put together, were the most terrible Pearl had ever spoken. They echoed off the welcome sign.

Victoria's arms fell to her sides. She looked a bit stunned, as if someone had tossed cold water in her face. Pearl took a step toward her. "Uh, gee, I didn't—" Pearl started to say, but that chugging sound suddenly grew louder. Ben grabbed her arm.

"It's coming closer," he warned. Pearl whipped around.

A black truck had turned off the highway and was speeding toward them. Its brightly painted logo read, BYE-BYE, BUGS.

15

THE VACUUMATOR

Pearl ran into the middle of the road. Half her brain said, "Don't do it. You'll get flattened like a pancake." But the other half of her brain, the half with the louder voice, yelled, "*Save the fairies!*"

"Pearl!" Ben hollered. He reached out to grab her, but he wasn't quick enough. Once she'd set her mind to something, Pearl operated on one hundred percent pure determination. Her goal—keep the exterminator from reaching Buttonville.

The truck barreled toward her. She couldn't see the driver's face through the dirty, bug-splotched windshield. Headlights flashed at her. A horn blasted its warning. Despite the looming danger, she stood her ground, waved her arms above her head, and shouted, "*Stop!*"

The truck veered around her. Ben and Victoria jumped aside as the truck careened over the sidewalk. Brakes screeched, and the scent of burning rubber polluted the air. The truck came to a dead stop just inches from the Buttonville welcome sign. The engine sputtered, then went quiet.

I did it, Pearl thought, smiling at her accomplishment. But when the driver's head popped out the window and she saw the look on his face, she wanted to run in the other direction.

"Hey, kid, what are you doing? Are you crazy?" The door flew open, and the driver slid out. He was a very short man with thick arms like a weight lifter's. His overalls were blue, and his name tag read BUG GUY. "Better not be any damage," he grumbled, adjusting the pair of safety glasses that sat on his forehead. He stomped around the truck, kicking the tires and looking for dents. Then he climbed onto a rear wheel and began to inspect an odd contraption that sat in the truck's bed. It looked like some kind of machine, with a barrel-sized clear canister, a bunch of switches and buttons, and a long vacuum tube.

"The Vacuumator," Ben whispered to Pearl. She nodded.

"You have me to thank," Victoria said proudly. "I'm the one who called him. *I'm* saving the day."

Pearl wanted to tell Victoria that she wasn't *saving* the day. She was totally ruining it. But Pearl kept that comment to herself. She still felt bad about having said those other mean words.

Bug Guy seemed satisfied that nothing had broken. He stepped off the wheel, wiped his hands on his overalls, and frowned at Pearl. "Do your parents know you're playing in the middle of the road?"

"I wasn't playing," Pearl said. "I wanted to stop you. We don't need your help anymore."

"But I'm supposed to catch some killer bees," Bug Guy said.

"The killer bees are gone," Ben told him.

"Huh?" Victoria put her hands on her hips. Sunlight glinted off her blue braces as she spoke. "But

we just saw them on Main Street. What makes you think they're gone?"

"We saw them leave," Pearl replied.

Bug Guy reached into his pocket. "Don't be so sure. Killer bees are real good at hiding." He pulled out a green licorice rope and took a bite.

Pearl's legs stiffened. Would the fairies smell the candy and come swarming? That would be the absolute worst thing that could happen! "Uh, I wouldn't eat that if I were you."

"Why not?" Bug Guy asked.

"Candy's not healthy," Ben said, stepping closer to the man. "It can cause diabetes, and obesity, and..."

"And ringworm," Pearl added.

Ben gave her a weird look. "Yeah, and ringworm. Also, it can make you hyper, so you shouldn't eat it if you're driving and operating heavy equipment."

"What are you talking about?" Bug Guy spoke with his mouth full. "This is a special gluten-free, low-calorie licorice. It's practically good for you."

"Does it have sugar?" Pearl asked.

"Of course it has sugar. Wouldn't taste good

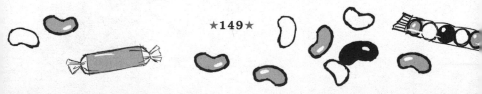

without sugar." He took another bite. Pearl and Ben looked at the sky. Sunny and blue, with no signs of churning clouds. Not yet, anyway.

Victoria, in her usual snoopy way, had climbed onto the truck's tailgate and was peering into the back. "How does this thing work?" she asked.

Bug Guy proudly puffed out his chest. "Well, the Vacuumator is my own invention. It's patent pending." He pointed to the glass barrel. "That's for vermin containment and observation." Then he pointed to the hose. "That's what sucks up the vermin. I've got all different sizes of nozzles. Got one big enough for rats and bats. And got one small enough for fleas. I even got one big enough for burglars. I figure police departments all over the world will want one." He showed her the end of the hose. "But I

put on the medium-sized nozzle, which should be just right for killer bees. And this here starts the suction." He pushed a button, and the Vacuumator started rumbling. "I'll show you." He aimed the hose at a pebble. In a flash, the pebble disappeared and reappeared inside the canister.

Pearl and Ben had inched forward to see what all the fuss was about. "What do the other buttons do?" Ben asked.

"That one is the off button. And that one spits the vermin back out, but that's only for relocation. We wouldn't want to relocate your swarm of killer bees. They'll have to be destroyed, of course, to make the world a safer place."

"Do you have a nozzle big enough for a dragon?" Victoria asked. She beamed a wicked smile at Pearl.

"Killer bees *and* dragons?" Bug Guy said with a snort. "What kind of town is this?" He took another bite of licorice. Pearl shuffled nervously. She'd never seen green licorice before. Although the sky was still clear, she was getting a very bad feeling.

"What flavor is that?" she inquired.

"Kiwi," he replied.

Both Ben and Pearl gasped.

"You want a piece?" Grasping both ends of the rope, he stretched it until it broke. A fruity scent filled the air, followed by high-pitched humming. A small cloud appeared above the tree line, swirling and churning and heading straight for them.

"Killer bees!" Victoria screamed.

Bug Guy dropped his licorice. "Push the button! Push the button!" he hollered as he pulled the vacuum hose out of the truck.

"No, *don't* push the button!" Pearl and Ben cried.

But Victoria's stubby fingers were already reaching for it, and before Pearl or Ben could stop her, the Vacuumator roared to life. Bug Guy slid his safety glasses over his eyes, raised the hose like a sword, and hollered, "Take cover!"

While Victoria crawled under the truck, Pearl lunged at the Vacuumator, and Ben lunged at Bug Guy. But their efforts were too late. The fairy swarm dive-bombed the kiwi-flavored licorice, and with swift aim, Bug Guy sucked them right out of the air.

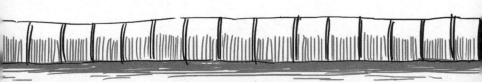

"Got 'em!" he shouted, just as Pearl reached and pressed the off button. The engine shut down and the suction stopped. But it was too late. "Got every last one of them! Bye-bye, bugs!"

Ben climbed into the back of the truck and peered into the canister. Pearl didn't want to look. What if the fairies were hurt? What if they were...dead? She couldn't bear seeing such horror. She closed her eyes and grimaced, waiting for Ben to deliver the news. "Are they...?"

"It looks like they're okay," he reported.

Pearl almost burst into tears. She climbed in next to him. Indeed, the fairies were flying around inside the container. They seemed a bit dazed, because they kept bumping into one another, but that was to be expected after what they'd been through. "Do you see Twanabeth?"

"There she is," Ben said, pressing a finger to the glass. Twanabeth had separated from the swarm and was waving and yelling at the apprentices. But without a creature calculator, they had no idea what she was saying.

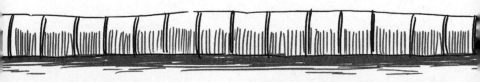

"How do we get them out of there?" Pearl whispered. The glass container didn't have a lid or an opening, other than the one for the vacuum hose, which was attached with a metal ring and bolts.

"If we push the relocation button, the fairies will shoot back out," Ben suggested.

Pearl looked over her shoulder at Bug Guy, who was wiping dirt from his licorice pieces. "But if we let them out, he'll go after them again."

"Right. I wonder..." Ben rubbed the back of his neck. "The vacuum hose is pretty long. If we could get this truck to the hospital, we could push the relocation button and shoot the fairies through a window into the Fairy Lounge."

"Brilliant," Pearl said. "But how—?"

"What's a fairy lounge?" Victoria interrupted. She'd crawled out from under the truck and was trying to squeeze between Ben and Pearl. Pearl tried to ward her off with some sharp elbow jabs, but Victoria threw her weight into the battle and broke through. "Those bees look weird." She was about to press her face against the glass. Fortunately, Ben was quicker.

"Oh no, you don't," he said, snatching her glasses off her face.

"Hey, give those back!" she complained.

"If you want them, come and get them." Ben

jumped out of the truck. Then he waved the glasses, trying to entice her away from the fairies. It worked. Victoria chased him around the welcome sign. Pearl stood in the truck's bed. What should she do? She glanced through the truck's back window. The keys were still in the ignition. Could she drive the truck to the hospital? She'd never driven before, but how hard could it be?

"Okay, kids, time for you to run along." With his mouth full of licorice, Bug Guy curled the hose into the truck. Then he grabbed the driver's-side door. "Gotta take those nasty killer bees back to the shop to be exterminated."

Pearl needed a distraction. Something that would lure Bug Guy away.

A yellow tennis ball rolled past the truck.

16

CAT AT THE WHEEL

The yellow tennis ball rolled into the middle of the road, leaving a glistening trail of slobber on the pavement. Ben, who'd been wrestling Victoria for possession of her glasses, froze in a half nelson and gawked. "Uh-oh," he said.

Victoria broke free and grabbed her glasses from his hand. "If you scratched my lenses, I'm gonna tell my mom, and you'll get into so much—" With her glasses back in place, she stopped talking and stared, slack-jawed, at the forest, from whence the tennis ball had emerged. Color drained from her face.

Pearl knew, without turning around, that a pair

of glowing red eyes were looking out from between the trees. She could hear the familiar thumping of a large tail. She smiled. Even if she'd gotten a wish from a genie in a bottle, no better distraction could have been conjured at that very moment.

After quickly climbing out of the truck, Pearl ran into the road, picked up the soggy tennis ball, and threw it down Main Street.

"What are you doing?" Ben asked with alarm.

Although she and Ben were a team, there was no time to huddle and agree on a plan. The ball soared like a comet across the sky and landed with a *thunk* outside the Welcome Wagon office. It rolled past the bookstore and then the diner, and came to a stop right in front of the Dollar Store. Pearl cupped her hands and yelled, "Fetch!"

Like an overgrown, scale-covered, fire-breathing puppy, Metalmouth bounded from the woods. "Oh goody, goody, goody," he said, his tongue hanging out. "We're gonna play fetch."

When it came to odd sightings in Buttonville, a galloping dragon certainly beat a swarm of killer

bees. Buildings shook, lampposts swayed, and pigeons scattered as Metalmouth charged into town. Steam spouted from his nostrils, fogging up windows.

Bug Guy forgot all about his job and his truck. He yanked his safety glasses off his head. "What in the blazes?" He took a few hesitant steps down the road. "Is that a—?"

"A dragon!" Victoria said, pushing Ben out of her way. "I knew it!" She took off at a full sprint.

"Hey, little girl!" Bug Guy called. "Maybe you shouldn't get too close!" But he didn't heed his own advice. He hurried after Victoria. "The other bug guys ain't gonna believe this."

A fire hydrant cracked open as Metalmouth's tail whacked it, releasing a geyser of water.

"I can't believe this is happening," Ben said.

"It was the only way to get rid of Victoria and Bug Guy." Pearl jumped into the driver's seat. She touched the key. She'd never driven anything before, not even a lawn mower, because her family didn't have a lawn. "I don't know what to do. Ben!"

He snapped out of it. "I've only driven cars in

video games," he told her as he hurried toward the truck.

"Then you can drive this one." She wasn't sure that was true, but it was worth a try. Persuading Ben to do things that made him uncomfortable had become one of her best skills.

"But it's against the law." He started wringing his hands. "Ten-year-olds aren't supposed to drive."

"Ten-year-olds aren't supposed to do a lot of things, but look at us. We're amazing!" She hoped the pep talk was working.

Ben hesitated. "We could get into huge trouble. And I thought—"

"Yeah, I know. I said I'm sick of being called a troublemaker, but I don't care anymore. The fairies need our help, and that's way more important than what people call me."

Up the street, the tennis ball had rolled into a gutter, and Metalmouth was trying to fish it out with one of his long claws. Victoria and Bug Guy were still mesmerized. Pearl smacked the steering wheel. "There's no time to argue. As soon as he gets the

ball, Metalmouth will run back here, and we won't be able to get away. Come on! Drive!"

She scooted across the bench seat. Ben climbed in and shut the door. Then, his hand trembling, he turned the key. The truck rumbled to life. Pearl glanced through the back window. The fairies were still flying around inside the canister. Ben seized the gearshift. "I can't believe I'm doing this. Hold on." He pushed the gear. The truck rolled forward and bumped right into the welcome sign.

"You have to go backward," Pearl told him.

"I know I have to go *backward*," he fumed. "I just don't know how."

"Maybe there's a button," she suggested. They looked at the dashboard. She fiddled with every knob and switch she could find. A spray of water coated the windshield. The wipers began to swoosh. The headlights flashed. The radio blared a country song. "Where is it?"

The driver's side door opened, and a voice said, "Scoot over."

"Mr. Tabby!" both Pearl and Ben cried as they made room for Dr. Woo's assistant.

"We're so glad to see you," Pearl said. She wanted to hug him. "We're trying to get the fairies to the hospital, but we don't know how to drive. And we have to go before Bug Guy notices we're taking his truck."

"I am well aware of the situation." Mr. Tabby turned off the radio, the wipers, and the headlights. "Seat belts," he instructed.

Pearl thought this was odd, considering that Mr. Tabby hadn't been concerned about seat belts while traveling between dimensions in the Portal. But she didn't argue. As soon as she and Ben were securely strapped in place, Mr. Tabby grabbed the gearshift. The truck backed away from the welcome sign. Ben groaned. The word *nicest* was dented.

"Mrs. Mulberry isn't going to like that," he said.

Mr. Tabby shifted again and drove the truck over the sidewalk and onto Main Street. Up at the other end, Metalmouth had finally collected his tennis

ball. He wagged his tail, hitting a lamppost so hard it toppled over. Victoria and Bug Guy didn't take their eyes off the dragon, so neither noticed that the truck was on the move.

Metalmouth, however, did notice. He looked down the street. Pearl reached her hand out the truck's window and waved. Seeing that his fetch partners were leaving, Metalmouth took to the sky, but his escape wasn't quick enough. Mrs. Mulberry stepped out of the Dollar Store, pointed, and screamed.

"Uh-oh," Pearl said.

Ben's knuckles went white as he gripped the dashboard. Mr. Tabby made a sharp turn onto Fir Street, leaving tire marks in the road. He might have been half cat, but he could handle the truck like a race car driver. Pearl's stomach lurched as the truck flew over a pothole. The poor fairies didn't even have seat belts!

They drove past the church and the closed gas station, then made a right onto Maple Street. Down the windy road they sped, leaving the town behind.

Pearl remembered the first time she and Ben walked the tree-lined street together, carrying a dragon hatchling in a cookie tin. Ever since, they'd walked there on Monday, Wednesday, and Friday mornings. Those had been some of the best mornings of her life.

As the hospital came into view, a large shadow passed overhead. Metalmouth soared gracefully over the lawn, then landed on the hospital's roof.

"The gate's open," Ben said with surprise. It was *never* open. Mr. Tabby kept it secured with a padlock, and he was the only one who carried the key. "Did you forget to close it?" Ben asked. He'd gotten in trouble for not locking the hospital's front door.

"I do not forget such things," Mr. Tabby said with a low growl. "I left it open as a time-saving measure."

Pearl wondered if this was true. Perhaps the doctor's assistant wasn't as perfect as he appeared.

Mr. Tabby drove up the gravel driveway and stopped abruptly in front of the entrance. They all scrambled out. While Ben unwound the vacuum hose, Mr. Tabby started inching it up the hospital's exterior wall, past the second, third, and fourth floors. Then past the fifth. "Wait," Ben said. "Don't you want to put them in the Fairy Lounge?"

"They are going to the tenth floor," Mr. Tabby said. "The rest of the fairies are waiting there."

"To the Portal?" Pearl was confused. "You're going to send them back? But how can you do that if Maximus is still in the Imaginary World? Won't he try to capture them? Doesn't he need their dust?"

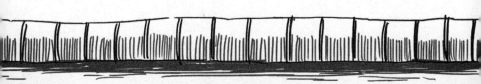

Mr. Tabby ignored her questions. He stood on the tiptoes of his polished shoes, stretching his entire body as he continued to push the vacuum hose higher and higher. Pearl climbed onto the tailgate. The fairies seemed wobbly, but they'd survived the crazy drive. When the hose reached the tenth floor, a window opened and a pair of furry hands emerged and grabbed the hose, pulling the nozzle inside.

"Now," Mr. Tabby told Pearl. She pressed the relocation button.

The Vacuumator's engine hummed, and then a *whoosh* sounded. The fairies swirled into a clump and were sucked out of the canister. In a matter of moments, the clump made its way up the tube and through the tenth-floor window. Mission accomplished! A furry hand reached out and waved. The vacuum tube tumbled to the ground.

Pearl pressed the off button. She threw her arms around Ben. "We did it!" she said. "We saved the fairies!"

"I'm so glad Mr. Tabby knows how to drive," Ben said with a grin. But the joyful moment burst like a

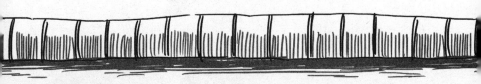

bubble as a police siren rose in the distance. "Uh-oh. I wonder if your aunt is looking for a stolen truck. Or a dragon. Or both!"

"Follow me," Mr. Tabby instructed. He didn't bother to move the truck or lock the front gate. Nor did he bother to bolt the hospital's front door after they'd all run inside.

Why is he forgetting all his rules? Pearl wondered as Mr. Tabby led them straight to the back stairwell. A bad feeling took hold of Pearl. Something big was about to happen. Ben frowned, looking equally worried as they followed Mr. Tabby to the tenth floor.

And when they stepped into the Portal room, the very thing Pearl was worried about—the worst thing that could possibly happen that summer— came true.

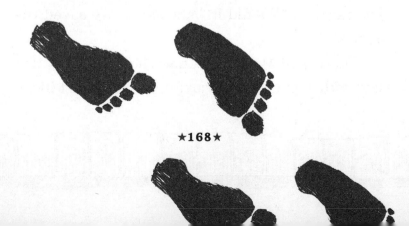

17

MOVING DAY

The tenth floor was usually empty, with just a switchboard on the far wall and a switchboard operator sitting on a stool. But when Pearl and Ben entered, they found the room crowded with boxes, crates, and a huge pile of suitcases. Dr. Woo's massive carved desk was there, too, and Metalmouth's metal nest. Pearl began to fidget. When Dr. Woo traveled to the Imaginary World, she took her medical satchel, nothing more. Why had all this stuff been brought upstairs?

And why was the room full of so many familiar faces? Aside from the fairies, who sat in the fairy trap, eating jelly beans, both Violet and Vinny were there. They stood next to the switchboard, sharing a bag of oats. The sasquatch was there, busily arranging suitcases into matching color stacks.

But most of the room was taken up by Metalmouth, who'd squeezed through a window and was bouncing his tennis ball. "Hiya, Pearl! Hiya, Ben!"

"Hello, little daaaaarlings," Violet said with a wave. Vinny snorted. The sasquatch stuck a suitcase on its head.

"Hi," Ben said.

Pearl could barely speak. She walked across the glittery floor and stopped next to a large red suitcase. A tag hung from its handle: PROPERTY OF EMERALD WOO. A big suitcase was only necessary if

someone was planning a *long* trip. Pearl swallowed hard. When she managed to find her voice, it was small and breathy. "Dr. Woo's...*leaving?*"

"Yes," Mr. Tabby said. "Dr. Woo is leaving Buttonville."

"What?" Ben's voice cracked. "You can't be serious."

"We're *all* leaving," Metalmouth said. "It's because of that bad guy, Maximus Steele. He's the reason we have to move again!" He bellowed so loudly a flame shot from his mouth and singed the nearby wall. The fairies shrieked, then went back to munching jelly beans.

"Calm dooooown," Violet said. Her hooves clacked as she waddled across the floor. She patted the dragon's front paw. "I know you're tired of moving, sweetie, but we have no other choice. We've got to close this Portal location right quiiiiick."

"Right quiiiiick," Vinny echoed, his mouth full of half-chewed oats.

"Why do you have to close it?" Ben asked. He looked anxiously at Mr. Tabby, as did Pearl. Would the grumpy assistant ignore the question?

To their surprise, Mr. Tabby cleared his throat, then offered an explanation. "Dr. Woo possesses the only legal contract to operate the Portal. Thus, the

Portal can deliver the doctor and her guests to any place in the Imaginary World. However, it only returns to one location in the Known World, and that location is wherever Dr. Woo lives. Which, at the moment, is Buttonville."

"We used to live in Iceland," Metalmouth said. "I liked it up there. Lots of warm, steamy volcanoes." The sasquatch grunted, as if in agreement, then began to make a new stack of brown suitcases.

"I don't miss it," Violet said. "Those lava rocks were hard on my hooooooves." She hurried back to her brother's side and began eating oats again.

Frustration filled Pearl, from the tips of her leprechaun shoes to the top of her blond head. She wanted to grab all the suitcases and throw them out the window. She'd do *anything* to keep Dr. Woo from moving. "I still don't get it," she said. "Why does Dr. Woo have to leave Buttonville? If this is about Mrs. Mulberry and Victoria and Bug Guy seeing Metalmouth, we can fix that. Ben will come up with a good cover story. Right, Ben?"

"Yeah," he said. "I'll tell them the dragon is a

robot that escaped from a Hollywood movie set."

Pearl smiled. "That's a good one. They'll believe him. See, you don't have to leave."

Mr. Tabby smoothed the ends of his mustache. "This has nothing to do with Metalmouth's game of fetch on Main Street. Do try to follow along so we can eliminate any unnecessary questions." He waited for their full attention, then proceeded. "In order to protect the Imaginary World, Dr. Woo must keep a low profile. There are always loathsome individuals who would take advantage of the Portal, most especially—"

"Maximus Steeeeele," Vinny and Violet bleated.

"He followed us from Iceland," Metalmouth said. "He's super sneaky."

Mr. Tabby growled softly. "Indeed, Steele is a hunter with superb tracking skills. And though he does not possess leprechaun shoes, he has trained himself to walk without detection. Soon after we moved to this abandoned factory, he crept inside, stole a vial of fairy dust, and summoned the Portal. It was enough dust for a one-way trip.

He's been in the Imaginary World ever since."

"It's Vinny's faaaaault," Violet said. She punched her brother in the shoulder. "He took a snack break."

"My fault?" Vinny shrugged. "I got hungry. So sue meeeee."

Violet yanked the bag of oats from his hand. "You're always taking snack breaks. You're supposed to watch the Portal at niiiiight!" She lowered her head and butted him with her horns.

"You take snack breaks, tooooo!" He lowered his head and was about to butt her back when a voice interrupted.

"Vinny is not to blame." All eyes turned to the door as Dr. Woo entered. She set a crate and an empty birdcage on the floor. "The Portal is my responsibility, and I must make things right." She looked at Pearl and Ben. "Will you give me a hand?" She wedged the door open with a small piece of wood. The apprentices followed her to the stairwell, which was crowded with all the stuff from her office. While Pearl wheeled a skeleton of a two-headed serpent, Ben carried a stack of boxes into the Portal room. Mr. Tabby grabbed the last few items.

"And the rest of the hospital?" Dr. Woo asked Mr. Tabby, wiping dirt from her lab coat.

"All taken care of," he told her.

"Excellent," she said. She smiled at Pearl and Ben. "I assume you two are feeling a bit surprised and confused." They nodded. "I had hoped to stay much longer. Buttonville is such a nice little town. And you've turned out to be better apprentices than I'd ever expected." Her smile faded. "But my time here has come to an end. Max will be arriving soon, and when he does, I will close this Portal location forever."

Pearl groaned. "Forever?"

"Wait..." Ben furrowed his brow. "Maximus Steele is coming *here*?"

"Yes," Dr. Woo said calmly.

"When?" Ben asked.

Mr. Tabby glanced at his pocket watch. "He could arrive at any moment."

Metalmouth tried to hide his face under his paws. "I don't like waiting. Tell me when it's over."

"But how can he get here?" Ben asked. "He doesn't have any fairy dust."

At that moment, Pearl realized that someone was missing. "Twanabeth," she said. She hurried to the fairy trap and peered inside. Some of the fairies were fast asleep, while others were still eating. But a crown-wearing, green-haired fairy was nowhere to be seen. "You sent her back?"

"Yes," Dr. Woo said. "You see, being stuck on a roof with no ladder is okay for my enemy, but it is terrible for me. If the fairies continue to stay here in the Known World, they cannot make magical fairy dust, and I have a limited supply, which will soon run out. If the fairies cannot replenish the dust, I cannot travel freely to help the creatures. My work will end, and many will suffer. And the fairies would be trapped here forever. And so, we must lure Max off the roof."

"You mean you've got to get him out of the Imaginary World?" Ben asked. "But how?"

Mr. Tabby's irises flashed. "The best way to catch a rat is with cheese."

"Cheese is goooood," Vinny bleated. With his sister still hogging the bag of oats, he'd begun to chew on an old shoe.

"Cheese?" Pearl asked. This plan was getting more confusing by the second. "But what does Twanabeth have to do with cheese?"

"What Mr. Tabby means is that we needed bait. Which is why I sent Twanabeth to find Max. She is carrying a message for him." Dr. Woo sat on a crate. Sensing a story was about to be told, Pearl and Ben gathered closer. "A few days ago, Mr. Tabby, Metalmouth, and I flew back to Iceland. I'd left a few things behind that I needed to retrieve. One of those items was a photo that I'd taken years ago of the reclusive Nemean lion."

"He was scary," Metalmouth said. "He bit off the doctor's finger!"

Dr. Woo held up her hand. "Yes, he did bite my finger. He thought that I'd come to hurt him."

"But you'd never hurt anything," Pearl said softly.

"The lion was acting on instinct when he bit and scratched me." She pointed to the scars on her face

and neck. "The claws of a Nemean lion are sharper than a sword and can cut through armor. Its golden fur is impervious to attack. I wouldn't have gone near him, but Max forced the encounter." Her sigh was long and weary, as if the memory brought great sadness.

Pearl tried to breathe as quietly as possible, not wanting to miss a single word. Ben held perfectly still. Violet and Vinny stopped chewing. Metalmouth's and Mr. Tabby's ears perked up. The sasquatch stopped stacking, and the fairies pressed against the side of the fairy trap, waiting for the story to continue.

"Max and I were working as apprentices to my grandmother Diamond Woo. We had just finished delivering cold medicine to a leprechaun family when Max disappeared without a trace. We were worried, of course. He'd never taken off before, and we had no idea what had happened to him. Days later, a call came in that the Nemean lion was in trouble. Grandmother and I found the lion in a trap, with Max trying to take one of its claws. Grandmother attempted to reason with Max, but his mind was poisoned with greed. Fortunately, Vinny arrived in the Portal and wrestled Max to the ground. Trying to help, I opened the trap. The lion lashed out at me." She looked at her hand. "That was one of the last times Max worked as our apprentice."

"So the photo of the lion is going to be some kind of bait?" Ben asked. "I don't get it."

"The lion represents a huge loss to Max. It was a creature that I took from him. And he has never forgotten. Now I've taken something else that he wants—the fairies. I wrote a message on the back of the photo. It says, 'You can't have them.' He will not be able to resist such a challenge. Twanabeth will allow herself to be caught. She will shed enough fairy dust for Maximus to summon the Portal."

Dr. Woo stood, her voice growing louder as she made the following proclamation. "Maximus Steele will come here ready for a hunt, but we will become the hunters. We will defeat him once and for all, and when we do, his days in the Imaginary World will be over!"

18

A STEELE TRAP

Dr. Woo had masterminded a four-pronged attack to defeat Maximus Steele.

Prong One: Fairy Strike. As soon as Maximus stepped out of the Portal, Dr. Woo would release the fairies, and they would distract him with fairy bites. Before her departure, Twanabeth had ordered her fairies to help the doctor. They had agreed.

Prong Two: Dragon Pounce. Once Maximus was distracted, Metalmouth would spring into the air and capture the hunter in his big paws.

"I don't wanna do that," Metalmouth grumbled, scooting back into a corner.

"Your pacifist tendencies are admirable," Mr. Tabby said. "But, for once, we need you to act like a dragon. Muster some of the ferocity that pulses through the veins of your species."

"I don't wanna pulse," Metalmouth said.

"Why not think of it as a game of fetch?" Ben suggested. "Pretend that Maximus is a big yellow tennis ball."

Metalmouth's tail thumped. "Oh boy, oh boy, I'm gonna play fetch."

Dr. Woo patted Ben's shoulder. "Wise suggestion," she said.

Prong Three: Net Toss. Mr. Tabby riffled through a crate, then removed a Sasquatch Catching Kit. Upon seeing the kit, the sasquatch grunted unhappily and hid behind Metalmouth.

"It is not for you," Mr. Tabby said as he opened the kit and pulled out a net. "Once Metalmouth has pounced on Maximus, Vinny and Violet will throw this over his head. I will secure the ends so Maximus can't escape." He handed the net to Vinny.

Then came the supersad part. The plan ended with Dr. Woo, Vinny, Violet, Metalmouth, the sasquatch, and the fairies escaping into the Portal.

That left Pearl, Ben, and Mr. Tabby to deal with Prong Four: Maximus Removal.

"You want us to *remove* him?" Ben scratched his head. "How are we supposed to do that?"

This part of the plan was worrisome to Pearl. Maximus was a muscular guy, and the last time they'd seen him, he'd carried a big knife. "I could call my aunt Milly. She could take him to jail."

"I appreciate your offer," Dr. Woo said. "But, unfortunately, Max hasn't broken any laws in the Known World." She took Pearl's hand. For someone about to face her enemy, her skin was surprisingly cool. "You and Ben do not have to assist with this plan. You have already been an enormous help by capturing the fairies. If you'd like to go home and avoid this unpleasant situation, please do so with my blessing."

"No way," Pearl said with a stomp of her foot. "I'd never go home, not now. This is important, and I want to help."

"Me too," Ben said. Pearl hadn't needed to nudge or encourage him. His expression was resolute. "We're staying."

"Very well," Dr. Woo said, releasing Pearl's hand. "Then help you shall."

Pearl grinned proudly. They were a team. No doubt about it.

"Maximus Removal will proceed as follows." Mr. Tabby began to pace. "Once Maximus is netted, the apprentices and I will carry him from the building. We will deposit him on the front lawn and release the net, and where he goes after that is none of our concern. Good riddance, I say."

"He better not stay in Buttonville," Pearl said.

"As long as I am not here, he will not stay," Dr. Woo assured her.

"But, Mr. Tabby? How come you're not escaping into the Imaginary World with the others? Is it because you'll turn into a cat?" Ben asked.

"I will remain in the Known World to search for a new location," Mr. Tabby explained. "I need to find a home for Dr. Woo so she can continue her important work."

"Only Imaginary creatures are allowed to live in the Imaginary World," Dr. Woo said. "Imaginary creatures exist under different laws of time and physics. I can visit for a while, but if I stayed there long-term, the effects on my human body would be detrimental. Likewise, Maximus can only stay there temporarily. It is another reason why he needs fairy dust."

"When you find a new home, will you call us? Or send a letter?" Ben asked.

"Can we come and visit?" Pearl imagined a slumber party with sleeping bags for her, Ben, and the sasquatch. Metalmouth wouldn't want to watch a scary movie, so she'd bring something funny, and lots of microwave popcorn.

Dr. Woo didn't answer. She looked out the window, a faraway expression settling in her eyes.

"Perhaps you should take this time to say your good-byes," she said, her voice hushed.

Pearl cringed. It felt as if Metalmouth had pounced on her chest. She didn't like good-byes. She didn't want to say them. Her heart began to pound. Her palms got clammy. "Drat," she muttered. And that was when thunder rumbled.

"Portal arriving!" Violet announced. The switchboard lit up. Violet stuck her headset over her goat ears and pushed a few buttons. "The Portal pilot reports there are two passengers—one human, one fairy."

"It is time," Mr. Tabby said.

Everyone scurried to the edges of the room. The Portal's arrival was a familiar sight to Pearl and Ben. The wind usually began as a wisp, then built into a tornado as the transportation device touched down. But this time was different. It was as if the Portal knew that one of its passengers was evil. Lightning bolts hit the roof, causing tiles to fall off. Thunder shook the building, toppling the switchboard itself. Violet shrieked, jumping out of the way. Pearl and Ben clung to each other as hurricane-force wind filled the room, roaring like a Nemean lion.

Pearl held an arm over her face, protecting her eyes from the swirling glitter.

"Everyone, get ready!" Dr. Woo hollered.

Dr. Woo grabbed the fairy trap, ready to release the fairies. Ben crouched next to Metalmouth, in case he needed encouragement to fetch. Violet, Vinny, and Mr. Tabby stood together, the net in Vinny's hands. Pearl didn't know what to do. She wasn't needed until the end of the four-pronged attack. Likewise, the sasquatch had nothing to do, so she grabbed its hand. It grunted at her. Glitter was stuck all over its fur, like an art project gone haywire.

The instant the Portal touched down, Twanabeth flew out of the swirling wind and began squeaking frantically. Mr. Tabby pulled his creature calculator from his vest pocket.

"Have fear, have fear, Maximus is here!" Twanabeth cried.

Pearl didn't want to *have fear*, but it hit her like a wave of cold water. Ben must have felt the same, because his lower jaw began to quiver. The anticipation was almost unbearable. Pearl was so glad her parents didn't know she was about to be a part of a four-pronged attack. They'd probably get a wee bit upset.

Maximus Steele emerged. The wind ceased, as did the thunder and lightning. The Portal vanished. For a moment, all was quiet on the tenth floor of Dr. Woo's Worm Hospital. The only visible movement was fairy dust settling back onto the floor.

He looked the same as when they'd last seen him in the griffin king's den. Tall and muscular, with a chiseled jaw and short dark hair. He wore a pith helmet, a khaki shirt, cargo pants, and sturdy black boots. A rope and a knife hung from his belt. His eyes darted, taking in the situation.

"Now!" Dr. Woo cried. She opened the fairy trap. The sugar fairies streamed out, a blur of beating wings and kicking legs.

"Bite him, bite him, bite and fight him!" Twanabeth ordered. Leading the charge, she and her fairies flew at their target. To Pearl's surprise, Maximus didn't cover his face or duck out of the fairies' path. Instead, he reached into the pockets of his cargo pants and tossed some items onto the floor. Jelly beans! The scent of kiwi filled the room. The swarm halted. Then, with squeals of delight, the fairies dove for the candies. Even Twanabeth couldn't resist. Maximus reached into his pocket again and pulled out a chocolate bar, which he tossed into the mix. With a happy grunt, the sasquatch plopped itself amid the fairies and began eating its prize.

Prong One: failure!

Dr. Woo whipped around and pointed at her dragon. Metalmouth seemed to have forgotten his role, or else he was too scared to move.

Ben gave him a shove. "Fetch!" Ben hollered. But

just as that word shot out of Ben's mouth, Maximus's hand slipped under his shirt and reappeared with a yellow tennis ball, which he tossed to the opposite end of the room.

The dragon's tail thumped. "Oh goody! I'm gonna play fetch! I'm gonna play fetch!" The floorboards rattled as he bounded toward the ball. Maximus grabbed the rope that hung from his belt, expertly tied it into a lasso, aimed, and...

Pearl gasped. It was like watching a train wreck and not being able to stop it.

Thud!

Metalmouth flipped onto his side, his front paws tied together. "Aw, gee whiz," he complained.

Prong Two: failure!

Dr. Woo turned and pointed at Violet and Vinny. Clutching the net, they rushed forward, Mr. Tabby at their side. Like a quick-draw cowboy, Maximus reached into his back pocket and pulled out a handful of ivy vines. He threw the vines at the satyrs' hooves. Distracted by their favorite treat, both Violet

and Vinny stumbled, giving Maximus enough time to grab the net and toss it. He pulled the cord tight, capturing Violet, Vinny, and Mr. Tabby.

Violet hit her brother in the shoulder. "This is all your faaaaault."

"My faaaaault?"

Prong Three: failure!

Pearl was impressed. Maximus had come prepared. He'd guessed Dr. Woo's plan, and he'd outsmarted her. But what were they supposed to do now? The fairies and the sasquatch were eating. Metalmouth was incapacitated. Violet, Vinny, and Mr. Tabby were trapped. Ben's mouth hung open in surprise. Even Dr. Woo looked shocked, her face suddenly as pale as the moon.

Maximus smirked at Dr. Woo. "It appears you underestimated me."

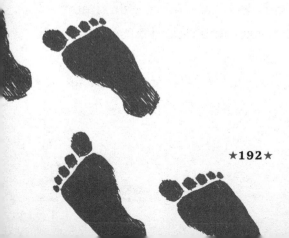

19

THE FOURTH PRONG

The tenth floor looked like a battlefield. Metalmouth lay on his side, groaning sadly. Violet, Vinny, and Mr. Tabby were wrapped so tightly in the net they couldn't budge an inch. The sasquatch had fallen asleep in a sugar stupor, and the fairies were still eating, paying not a smidge of attention to anything that was happening around them.

A mischievous twinkle danced in Maximus's eyes as he stood, hands on hips, facing Dr. Woo, Pearl, and Ben. "It's nice to see you again, Emerald. And your young apprentices."

Dr. Woo stepped protectively in front of Pearl and Ben.

For what felt like an eternity, she and Maximus stood in silence, staring at each other. No one dared interrupt. Dr. Woo and Maximus had been apprentices together. They'd been friends. But now they were enemies with completely different goals—one to protect and heal, the other to hunt and steal.

Maximus eyed the fairy trap. "Hand it over and we can be done with this charade," he said, reaching out his hand.

Dr. Woo wrapped her arms protectively around the trap. "I will never let you have the fairies. I will never let you return to the Imaginary World."

He laughed a deep belly laugh, as if that was the funniest thing he'd ever heard. "You won't *let* me?" He laughed again. It was such an eerie sound that the back of Pearl's neck got prickly. Then his expression went cold. "I won't take no for an answer."

"Get out of my hospital," Dr. Woo said through clenched teeth.

"Get out? But you so nicely invited me here." He

removed a photograph from his pocket. "This was your invitation, was it not? You sent this photo to remind me that I'd lost the Nemean lion. I hadn't forgotten, Emerald. I don't forget things like that." He took a step forward. "I won't lose again."

Ben jumped in front of Dr. Woo. "We called the police," he lied. "They'll be here any minute."

"Yeah," Pearl said. "My aunt's an officer, and she's on the way!"

Maximus froze. He raised an eyebrow. "Emerald would never get the police involved. She has too many secrets to protect."

"I have an entire world to protect," Dr. Woo said.

He folded his arms, and his tone suddenly grew friendly. "I have an idea. Why not join me? I could use a couple of apprentices. Think of what we could accomplish. Think of the wealth we could amass if we all worked together. What do you say, Emerald?"

Pearl was a big fan of questions, but why would Maximus bother asking such a stupid one? Of course Dr. Woo wouldn't help him. But just as Pearl thought this, Dr. Woo said a very surprising thing.

"Wealth?" She pushed both of her apprentices away, as if they suddenly meant nothing to her. "You know, I am a bit tired of never getting paid for my work. What do you have in mind?"

Pearl gasped. Was this really happening? Was Dr. Woo actually interested in working with Maximus Steele? *No. Never. Not in a million years!* She looked over at Mr. Tabby. His face peeked out from behind the netting. He didn't seem alarmed. In fact, he winked at Pearl.

Of course. This was a ruse. Dr. Woo was trying to buy time. But what could Pearl and Ben do with the extra time?

As Maximus launched into a long explanation about how they could form a partnership, Ben tugged on Pearl's sleeve. It was too risky to whisper or point, so he mouthed a word. She didn't understand. What was he saying? He mouthed it again, and again.

Vacuumator.

Oh, that was unbelievably brilliant! Bug Guy had told them there was a nozzle big enough for

burglars. Which meant it was big enough for poachers. But how could they get to the Vacuumator? It was outside.

As if reading Pearl's mind, Ben darted his gaze to her shoes.

Right! She was the only one in the room wearing leprechaun shoes, which meant she was the only one who could walk silently across the floor.

To give Pearl a chance to escape, Ben set about distracting Maximus. But instead of making up a story, he employed one of Pearl's favorite tactics. "So, Mr. Steele, why do you want to make a lot of money? What are you going to do with it? Is there something you want to buy? Do you get your clothes from a special hunting catalog? Did you feel bad when you hurt the rain dragon? Did you like being an apprentice? Is there any advice you can give me so I can be a better apprentice? Do you..."

Pearl slipped behind Metalmouth. Then she inched toward the door. Not a sound was made as she crept into the stairwell.

Even if she'd owned a pair of fairy wings, she

couldn't have flown any faster down those stairs. Her feet barely touched the steps. Floor nine, floor five, floor two. She raced up the hallway, through the EMPLOYEES ONLY door, into the lobby, and onto the front stoop. How much time would pass before Maximus noticed that she was gone? Would he come after her?

The truck was still parked next to the building. She climbed into the truck's bed and searched through the nozzles. *Hurry, hurry, hurry*, she told herself. A small nozzle. A medium-sized nozzle. There it was, one big enough to fit over a person's head. She grabbed the vacuum hose and unscrewed the killer bee nozzle. Then, her hands shaking, she attached the big one. Maximus wouldn't hurt Dr. Woo, would he? They'd been friends. And he'd let Pearl and Ben bring Dr. Woo a griffin feather so she could be cured of Troll Tonsillitis. That meant he cared about her. But he wanted those fairies. *Hurry, hurry, hurry.*

Just as Mr. Tabby had done, she inched the hose up the wall, aiming for the open window. Ben's

timing was perfect. He reached through the window and grabbed the hose, pulling it inside. Pearl dove at the machine and pressed the suction button.

The engine hummed and sputtered. And sputtered again. *Oh no!* This wasn't happening! Pearl kicked it. Her father sometimes kicked the washing machine when it acted up. More sputtering. "Start!" she screamed. As if the engine had heard her, it roared to life. The vacuum hose stiffened. Air began to swirl in the glass barrel. For a moment, Pearl wondered if it was big enough to hold Maximus. If not, would he get stuck in the tube?

She was about to run back inside when a heart-stopping scream rang from the tenth floor. It was the sound of a creature caught in a trap—a creature who thought he'd *never* be captured. When Maximus Steele had stepped out of the Portal, he'd been prepared for many things. He'd known about the sasquatch and the fairies, so he'd brought sweets. He'd known about Metalmouth, so he'd brought a tennis ball. And he'd known about the

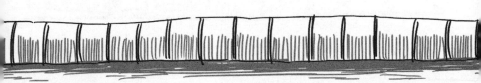

satyr brother and sister, so he'd prepared for them as well. But what he could never have anticipated was a machine that sucked up vermin of *all* shapes and sizes.

A giant lump appeared at the top of the hose. Then the lump slowly moved down the tube. It was like watching a boa constrictor swallowing a boulder. Inch by inch, foot by foot, it moved. The engine groaned and kicked into a higher gear. The lump had made it halfway down. Smoke began to rise from the machine as it overheated. Pearl feared the thing would explode. She backed away.

Then, with a final surge, Maximus shot out of the hose and into the container. Like the fairies before him, he was a bit stunned at first. He rubbed his head. He blinked quickly. Stuck in a squatting position, he pressed his hands against the glass and glared at Pearl. He pounded his fists and hollered. Pearl didn't need a creature calculator to translate. He  was *mad!* The barrel rocked from side to side, but he couldn't break free. The Vacuumator hose fell from the window and landed beside the truck.

Ben popped his head out the window. "Pearl, hurry! We need your help."

Did she dare leave Maximus alone? The container seemed sturdy. He might end up with leg cramps, but he wouldn't suffocate, thanks to the airholes. She glared at him and hollered, "Now you know how it feels to be trapped!"

"Pearl!" Ben called again.

"Pearl Petal!"

This time it wasn't Ben calling. It was Mrs. Mulberry. She was stomping up the hospital driveway, with Victoria at her heels. "What are you doing with that truck?"

There was no time to waste. Pearl turned away, dashed back through the lobby, down the hallway, and to the staircase. She pumped her arms and legs. Her lungs began to burn as she gasped for air. It was way harder going *up* those nine flights. Just as she thought she might collapse, she burst onto the tenth floor.

The Portal had already been summoned. It swirled in the center of the room. Ben was untying Metalmouth's legs. Dr. Woo was untangling Violet, Vinny, and Mr. Tabby from the net.

"Mulberrys!" Pearl announced, trying to catch her breath. "Mulberrys!"

Mr. Tabby rose to his feet and smoothed his

pants and vest. Violet tried to adjust her beehive hairdo, which had gone a bit lopsided. Vinny didn't seem to care about his appearance. He tossed the net aside with an angry bleat.

Pearl ran to the window. Mrs. Mulberry and Victoria were standing next to the truck, staring in confusion at the man in the container. "Hurry! Hurry! Before they let him out!"

"Yes, we must hurry," Dr. Woo said. She shook the sasquatch awake.

They all worked together to get the boxes, crates, and suitcases into the Portal. Metalmouth carried the switchboard. The sasquatch pushed the carved desk. Everyone pushed the metal nest. Then Dr. Woo looked around. "It's time," she said. "It's time to say good-bye."

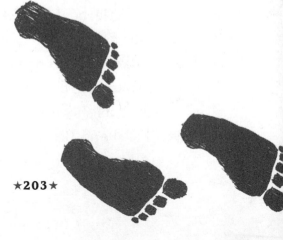

20

It was the saddest moment of Pearl's life. Her heart felt as heavy as a stone. She choked back tears. Even Ben's eyes got misty.

Vinny didn't bother saying anything. He just waved, then stepped into the Portal.

Violet gave Pearl and Ben each a kiss on the cheek. Her little beard tickled. "Good-bye, little darlings," she said with a sniff. She pulled a polka-dotted handkerchief from her pocket and dabbed her eyes. "Take care of your sweet seeeeelves." Her dress billowed as she hurried through the wind.

"Bye," Pearl and Ben called.

Twanabeth zipped around Pearl's head. Pearl covered her earlobes, but the fairy flew to the tip of Pearl's nose. Pearl cringed, expecting a painful bite, but her nose only tingled. And it felt warm, as if the sun were shining upon it. "Did she bite me?" Pearl asked.

"On the contrary," Dr. Woo explained. "That was a fairy kiss. They are very powerful."

Twanabeth kissed Ben's nose. "Nice girl, nice boy, saved the fairies, shout for joy!"

The other fairies shouted, "Hurray!" Then Twanabeth whistled, and her swarm followed her into the Portal.

It was the sasquatch's turn. Over the last few weeks, Pearl had complained an awful lot about all their sasquatch-related chores. The flea bath had been the worst. But until this very moment, she hadn't realized how attached to the big oaf she'd become.

"I'm going to miss our yoga sessions," she said, wrapping her arms around its waist. She got a bit of fur in her mouth, but she didn't mind.

Ben shook the sasquatch's hand. "Bye," he said. "It was really nice meeting you. Even though they have all those TV shows about you, I didn't think you existed." The sasquatch tousled Ben's hair. Dr. Woo tossed a chocolate bar into the Portal, and the sasquatch lumbered after it.

Which left Metalmouth.

Pearl gulped. "Thanks for taking us for a ride," she said. She tried to hug him, but it was next to impossible. He was way too big, and his scales were sharp and slippery. So she patted his front paw.

"Aw, gee," Metalmouth said, his ears flattening. "I don't like saying good-bye."

"Me neither," Ben said. Pearl stepped back to give Ben some room. She knew this would be especially difficult for him. "I'm gonna miss you," he whispered in the dragon's ear.

"I'm gonna miss you, too." A big, fat tear rolled down Metalmouth's cheek. Then the dragon pulled a tennis ball out from under one of his scales and gave it to Ben.

"Thanks," Ben said. As Metalmouth turned away,

Ben quickly wiped his eyes with his shirtsleeve. "I'll never forget you!" Ben called as the dragon entered the swirling wind.

"You better not," Metalmouth called back, and as he did, a flame shot out. "Oops. Sorry about that!"

During all the farewells, Mr. Tabby had been keeping watch at the window. "The Mulberry child has climbed into the truck and appears to be pressing buttons," he reported. "Dr. Woo, you must go."

Dr. Emerald Woo stood before Pearl and Ben, her long black hair blowing gracefully as the Portal waited to carry her away. "You are the best apprentices I've ever had," she said. Then she pulled two rolled certificates from her lab coat pocket. Each was tied with a ribbon. "I want you to have these. And these, too." She opened her medical satchel and pulled out their lab coats and time cards.

"Why are you giving us these?" Pearl asked.

"Because you may need them again."

"Really?" Ben asked.

"Does that mean...?" Pearl bounced on her toes. "Does that mean...?"

"It means that I would hate to lose the best apprentices I've ever had." She pulled them both into a hug. "Our paths shall cross again." She let

them go. The hem of her lab coat rippled as she slipped away.

Pearl and Ben waved until their arms grew heavy. The Portal disappeared. The fairy dust settled. All was quiet.

Except for the shouting. And the sound of an approaching siren.

Pearl, Ben, and Mr. Tabby leaned out the window. Victoria had apparently pressed the relocation button, because Maximus Steele was free. He'd climbed into the driver's seat of the truck. Mrs. Mulberry and Victoria pounded on the door.

"Who are you? Do you know Dr. Woo?" Mrs. Mulberry demanded.

"Where's the dragon?" Victoria cried.

The truck's engine started. Gravel spewed out from under the wheels as Maximus stepped on the gas.

"Hey! That's my truck!" Bug Guy hollered. He'd run all the way from town and was leaning against the open gate, trying to catch his breath. The truck barreled down the driveway and onto the road.

Officer Milly's police car did a 180-degree turn and followed the truck. Bug Guy started running again. "Hey! Come back here!"

"Hope that's the last we see of Maximus," Ben said as the truck disappeared around the bend.

Despite her sadness, Pearl snickered. "Maybe he'll become an exterminator."

"It seems the perfect fit for him," Mr. Tabby said with a sneer. Then he picked up the only suitcase that remained, and the former apprentices followed him downstairs. They reached the lobby just as Mrs. Mulberry and Victoria barged inside.

"I know that dragon lives on the roof!" Victoria said. "And we're going to find him!"

"Lead the way, Victoria," her mother told her. They pushed between Pearl and Ben, heading for the elevator. "I knew we'd get inside Dr. Woo's hospital. It was only a matter of time. We Mulberrys always get what we want!"

"Indeed," Mr. Tabby said. "But do you get what you deserve?"

The elevator doors opened, and Victoria and her

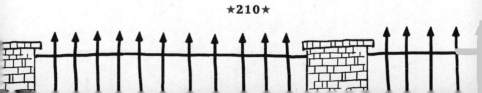

mother squeezed inside. "Push that button. And that button," Mrs. Mulberry ordered. "We'll find that dragon!"

Pearl and Ben watched as the elevator doors closed. So much energy had been spent trying to keep the Mulberrys from entering the hospital, and now they were about to explore every inch. But it didn't matter. There were no secrets to uncover. The Portal was gone. Everyone was gone. Pearl sighed.

Mr. Tabby opened a closet and removed a travel cloak, which he put on, and a hat.

"Where will you go?" Ben asked.

"I do not yet know. But I will find a new hospital for Dr. Woo. It may take days. It may take months." He patted his vest pocket, where the top of a glass vial peeked out. It was full of glittery yellow dust. "When all is ready, I will summon her."

He led them down the driveway, where a taxi was waiting. The driver opened the trunk and placed the suitcase inside. Mr. Tabby set his hat onto his head. Then he looked down at Pearl and Ben. "Despite the fact that I do not like training human apprentices, and that you two broke more rules than I choose to count, it has not been an entirely unpleasant experience. In fact, I would not object if Dr. Woo decides to work with you again." His nose twitched. "Do I detect the odor of sadness?"

Pearl frowned. "Sadness doesn't smell."

"Of course it does. And right now, young lady, you stink. So cheer up. Dr. Woo will return."

Then, without further ado, he slipped into the taxi. Pearl and Ben stood on the sidewalk, watching until the taxi disappeared around the bend. Pearl sniffed her shirt. "I don't really stink, do I?"

"No," Ben said. "But I feel sad, too."

Pearl grabbed the sign that was hanging from the gate.

WELCOME TO DR. WOO'S WORM HOSPITAL.
DR. WOO DOES NOT TREAT CATS, DOGS, PIGS, RATS,
SNAKES, TURTLES, FISH, FROGS, OR ANY
OTHER CREATURE THAT IS NOT A WORM.
DR. WOO SEES WORMS BY APPOINTMENT ONLY.
IF YOU DON'T HAVE AN APPOINTMENT,
KEEP OUT!

"I'm going to keep this as a souvenir."

Slowly, they started walking back toward town. Ben slung his lab coat over his shoulder. "Do you really think we'll see her again?" he asked.

"I sure hope so. Dr. Woo said we're the best apprentices she's ever had."

He shrugged. "Maybe she was just saying that to make us feel better."

"No way. We are the best. Look at all the things we did. We sneaked the sasquatch out of the senior center. We helped the lake monster feel less lonely, and we rescued Cobblestone from Button Island. We fixed the rain dragon's wound and helped her get a new horn. We saved the unicorn foal, and we cured Dr. Woo and the others of Troll Tonsillitis. Seriously, we're amazing."

"You're right," he said. "But what about everyone in town? They're going to blame you for the killer bees. They're going to call you a troublemaker."

"Who cares what they call me?" Pearl said. "I'm proud of myself. I'm proud of us."

"I'm proud of us, too." Ben bounced the tennis ball as they walked.

The Town Hall bell began to chime. As Pearl and Ben walked down the street, people emerged from their houses. The shopkeepers opened their doors. And everyone began to talk about the odd events of the day. The air filled with questions.

Pearl, however, had only one question on her mind. Her stomach had been growling something fierce. "Want to go to the diner and get something to eat?" she asked Ben.

"Yes. But—"

They looked at each other and, at the same time, said, "*No sugar!*"

SMALL TOWN GETS UNEXPECTED VISITOR

Not much happens in the rundown town of Buttonville. But last week, a handful of locals swear they saw an unusual creature running up the street.

"It was a dragon," Mrs. Martha Mulberry said. As the president of the Buttonville Welcome Wagon Committee, Mrs. Mulberry says it's her job to greet all newcomers when they come to town. "I tried to talk to it, but the nasty thing spat fire at me."

"I'm an expert on vermin," Bug Guy said. He works as an exterminator. "And that was the biggest pest I've ever seen. It was definitely a dragon."

Since the sighting, Buttonville has been flooded with tourists. "That dragon is the best thing that ever happened to this town," said Mr. and Mrs. Petal, owners of the local

Dollar Store. "We can barely keep our shelves stocked. The tourists are buying so much stuff."

But others are skeptical. "Dragons aren't real," said a boy named Ben Silverstein. "You'd have to be a little bit crazy to believe in dragons."

"They are real," said a girl named Victoria Mulberry. "And I'm going to prove it."

"She's been sitting on the roof every night with her camera," Mrs. Mulberry said about her daughter. "When that dragon flies by, she'll get a photo. And then everyone will see that we're not crazy."

"Yeah, but every time I get up there, someone takes the ladder away," Victoria said. "I bet it's that Pearl Petal. She's a troublemaker!"

Pearl Petal was busy with chores and could not be reached for comment.

CERTIFICATE OF MERIT
BEN SILVERSTEIN
IS HEREBY SKILLED IN THE ART OF
RESCUING SUGAR FAIRIES

CERTIFICATE OF MERIT
PEARL PETAL
IS HEREBY SKILLED IN THE ART OF
RESCUING SUGAR FAIRIES

PUT YOUR IMAGINATION ~ TO THE TEST ~

The following section contains writing, art, and science activities that will help readers discover more about the mythological creatures featured in this book.

These activities are designed for the home and the classroom. Enjoy doing them on your own or with friends!

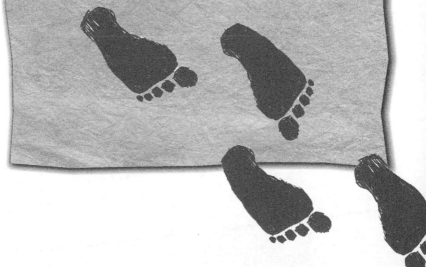

CREATURE CONNECTION
★ *Killer Bees* ★

Unfortunately, killer bees do not come from the Imaginary World. They are very real and can be quite dangerous.

Back in 1956, some scientists brought southern African bees to South America in an attempt to breed a better honeybee. They thought the southern African bees would be a good choice because they eat nectar and pollen, and make honey. But this experiment went awry. The African bees escaped quarantine, bred with local bees, and started a new, aggressive species that quickly spread throughout South and Central America.

These bees are called killer bees because they sometimes attack animals and people who stray into their territory. Their venom isn't more toxic than regular honeybees', but they attack in large numbers, and that is what makes them dangerous. And they can stay on the attack for up to twenty-four hours, making it difficult for their victim to escape!

It didn't take long for these bees to migrate beyond South and Central America. In 1990, a swarm of killer bees was found in Texas.

While they are dangerous to humans and animals, killer bees also pose a threat to honey production. As they spread to new territories, they breed with native bees, thus increasing the population of aggressive bees. Aggressive bees are difficult to farm for honey.

It seems that in our attempt to make a new type of bee, we messed things up. But hopefully, in the near future, we will find a better way to deal with these creatures.

STORY IDEAS

Pretend you are a scientist. You want to make a better ladybug. Ladybugs are very helpful to farmers because they eat aphids—bad bugs that destroy crops. You bring in a special bug from a faraway land to breed with local ladybugs, hoping to make them bigger so they can eat more aphids. But the result is not what you expected. What happens?

★ ★ ★ ★ ★

Imagine that you and your best friend are walking in the woods, and suddenly you hear a buzzing noise. You turn to find a swarm of killer bees coming right at you! What do you do? Can you find a place to hide? How do you survive?

ART IDEA

Can you create a new insect? Use this handy list and combine two or more to create your new bug. Feel free to add more bugs to the list.

beetle

bumblebee

butterfly

cockroach

flea

housefly

ladybug

mosquito

ant

wasp

hornet

SCIENCE CONNECTION
★ *Why Do Bee Stings Hurt?* ★

Has this ever happened to you? It's a lovely summer day, you're walking barefoot in the grass, and suddenly your toe feels like it's on fire?

Well, you've probably just stepped on a bee.

Not all bees have stingers, but those that do use them as a protection device. The stinger is filled with a substance called venom. The bees use the venom to subdue enemies.

In most cases, the sting is annoying and hurts for a little bit. There's a red welt and a white spot where the stinger entered the skin. When you pull out the stinger with tweezers or your fingernails, you'll probably start to feel better.

But in some cases, the sting is life-threatening. Some people are allergic to bee stings, and when stung, they have an allergic reaction called anaphylaxis. This means that the tongue and the throat begin to swell, making it difficult to breathe. Treatment is needed right away.

How does this happen?

Bee venom is able to destroy cells. When a person gets stung by a bee, the body releases histamine, which helps our immune cells reach the sting faster and begin the healing process. But for people who are allergic to bee stings, too much histamine is released and the body's reaction is extreme. People with bee-sting allergies often carry emergency medicine, to be on the safe side.

If you don't have an allergy to bees, don't be afraid to walk barefoot—it's one of the lovely joys in life. But it's always a good idea to check the grass and make sure that you're not stepping in an area where bees are collecting pollen.

CREATIVITY CONNECTION
★ *Create a Fairy* ★

In *The Fairy Swarm*, Mr. Tabby told Pearl and Ben that there are many kinds of fairies. Sugar fairies eat anything sweet. Burrowing fairies live underground. Bat fairies sleep upside down. Worker fairies do manual labor.

Using art supplies of your choosing, can you draw one of these fairies or make up your own sort of fairy? Imagine its clothes, its hair, and its wings. Does it live in a nest, a mushroom house, or a hole? Does it go barefoot or wear shoes?

Have fun!

CREATIVE WRITING CONNECTION

Ben and Pearl are done with their apprenticeships for the time being, but they have great hope that a day will come when they'll be reunited with Dr. Woo.

But what if Dr. Woo needs another apprentice, and what if that person is you?

It's your turn to write the story. Tell us all about the day when you discover that you've been chosen to be Dr. Woo's next apprentice.

A SPECIAL THANK-YOU TO MY READERS

I've loved writing this series. It's been so much fun exploring Buttonville and the old button factory. Ben, Pearl, Dr. Woo, and Mr. Tabby have all found a very special place in my heart. And Metalmouth is the kind of puppy that I would love to play fetch with.

When an author creates characters and spends years with them, as I have with this series, the characters become a part of the author's being. And although I'll move on to other stories, my characters will stay with me forever. After all, I breathed life into each and every one of them.

But so have you. You have also breathed life into my characters, because you've spent time with them, and thus, they've become a part of your being as well. And I hope that as you grow up, you will always remember Ben and Pearl, and the lovely time you all shared together.

Happy reading to you, dear friends, in both the Known and Imaginary Worlds.

Suzy Self

ACKNOWLEDGMENTS

Wow, this has been one of the best projects I've ever worked on, and I couldn't have done it without a remarkably creative team. Julie Scheina began this project with me, then gracefully passed the crown to Pam Garfinkel, who has been an amazing editor—thoughtful, respectful, and supportive. Christine Ma is the best copy editor in the world. And to the rest of the Little, Brown team, Victoria Stapleton, Alvina Ling, Sasha Illingworth, Marisa Finkelstein, Kristina Aven, Jenny Choy, Emilie Polster, Adrian Palacios, Renée Gelman, Rebecca Westall, Kristin Dulaney, Dave Epstein, Shawn Foster, Andrew Smith, and Megan Tingley, thank you.

Dan Santat never let this series down. His illustrations were always a joy to behold, and I'm so grateful to him. Michael Bourret, you know all the reasons why I'm crazy about you.

And to Bob, Walker, and Isabelle, you are the fairy dust in my world. You three inspire me to do my best and to keep stepping through that portal into Imaginary Worlds. And then to come back home again. I love you.

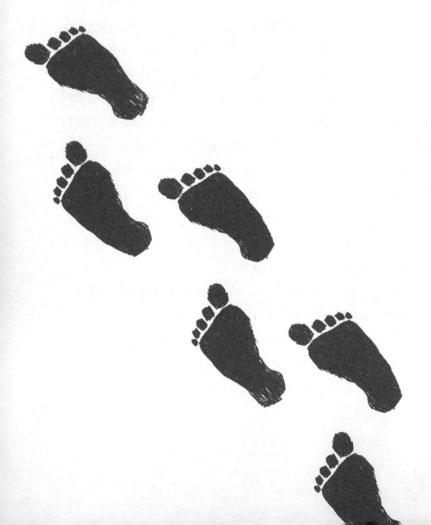

SUZANNE SELFORS is the author of the Imaginary Veterinary series, the Ever After High: A School Story series, the Smells Like Dog series, *Fortune's Magic Farm*, *To Catch a Mermaid*, and many other books. She lives at the edge of a grand forest, where she and her children have built many fairy houses. Her website is suzanneselfors.com.

DAN SANTAT is a children's book writer and illustrator, and a Caldecott Medal winner for *The Adventures of Beekle: The Unimaginary Friend*. He graduated from Art Center College of Design and lives in Southern California with his family, a rabbit, a bird, and one cat. His website is dantat.com.